# Escape the Chicken Coop

## A Novel Based on True Events

Leanette Lopez
S. L. Miles
(Book Discussion Guide included)

XULON PRESS

*For Tina V.,*

*You're the one who was "mad for me."*

## Author: Leanette Lopez

This book was a lifelong dream coming to pass in the heart of my coauthor S.L. Miles. Its conception came from a mutual friend, Cindy Paschall, who connected us knowing both our stories and our purpose in life. Our goal is for people to extract the poison of secrets that live inside by talking about it to one person or one million. I want to personally thank Martin Lopez for his tireless work in editing the manuscript. Thanks to the joy of my life, Kristen Lopez, the person who inspired her mommy to work for many hours. Thank you to my brothers and sisters-in-law, who were there for me always. I also want to thank Pastor Tim H., my friend, who prayed with me and talked to me throughout the difficult scenes I had to write. Thank you to my parents who loved me through. Thanks to my church, The Church on Strayer, in Toledo, Ohio for your love, fellowship and spiritual sustenance. I thank God for the personal crisis I endured during the writing of this book…it helped me dig deep into my own past and produce a novel I am sure will touch many souls.

Coauthor: S.L. Miles

Even though things were rough (to say the least) with my relationship with mom, I have come to an understanding that she did what she thought was best at the time. Can we choose who we fall in love with? She loved my dad. How hard is it to choose between the man you love and your child/children that all your natural instincts compel you to protect? What kind of turmoil do these choices cause in a person's heart and mind? As I sit with my Mom now that many years have passed I can still see the wall that she has put between us. She has been through many disappointments, physically and mentally. She tries now to make me feel like she cares and I know that she does but with the Alzheimer's she doesn't remember a lot of the last twenty years. But after my visits she always tells me that she loves me. I think that I was in my late thirties the first time that I remember my mom telling me that she loved me. It was an odd feeling to hear those words after so many years of waiting to hear them. It almost seemed like it didn't matter anymore. But it did! Now after years of pondering what ifs and what should have beens I have come to realize that my mom did the best that she could with what she had to deal with. And therefore I dedicate this book in her honor. I LOVE YOU MOM!

# Chapter 1

# *The chicken coop*

The wood burning stove smell was neutralized by the chilled air with the beginnings of winter. The wind blew in snow from an opened window and crystallized the edges of the old plank floor she sat on. Ann reached out and placed her hands on the warped splintered wood allowing the heat to escape her hand and make a melted print. The tingling cold breeze made her feel alive. Her big green eyes were filled with wonder. She wasn't allowed to leave the chicken coop and daydreamed of climbing a tree. The wind dried up the melted snow but the experience dried up her spirit. Later that night she would no longer feel alive, she was forever changed. She was four and her blueprint was formed.

It was November 1959. Ann's mother was giving birth to her brother John. Along with her siblings, Evan, George, Sadie, Joseph and Butch, Ann had to stay at grandma's house that night.

Grandma Novak loved taking care of the children. She lived in a nearby home for which Ann was grateful. Grandma enjoyed watching them orchestrate impromptu plays while she cooked them dinner. Before they ate she would have them each ask any question they wanted and to tell their own story. In stoking their curiosity and wonder, it made her feel youthful. She loved allowing her grandchildren to build tents with blankets and sleep on the floor. They liked feeling as though they were on an expedition. She gave them a flashlight to shine on each other at night. Children's books were left out in hopes they would read them.

Grandma was religious and liked taking them to Sunday school whenever she had them on the weekends. Ann will always remember the commitment she made in her heart when she was in one of the classes. What Ann found that weekend was beyond religion—it was a faith she would learn to seize with all her might. Although she was on the floor she was devoted to say her prayers before her eyelids became too heavy to stay open.

One by one they all fell asleep. Grandma walked in and turned off their flashlight and made sure they were all warm and covered. She thought she heard a disturbance outside but dismissed it as wild animals lurking in the night. It was a time of innocence where no one in the neighborhood needed to lock their doors.

As they were all sound asleep in their makeshift tents a stumbling dark figure snuck in the front door. He wanted one of the girls and the first one he found was Ann. She was sequestered from her grandma's in the middle of the night, he threw her over his shoulder as if she were a sack of potatoes, ran down the road and across the creek.

"Hold on Sadie." He staggered trying to keep his balance.

"Where are you taking me?" This was happening fast and Ann wasn't sure who took her.

The creek was semi-frozen from a premature winter storm. It made sluggish the flow of water. Tree branches were weighed down by icicles as if they were bowing to a majestic being. The branches glistened in the night with the moonlight reflecting on them. The trees rested on the snowy mountains of Wolford, Virginia.

A flicker of moonlight allowed her to catch a glimpse. *"Where are you taking me? Why are you taking me?"*

Ann can see the chilled air with each breath through his mouth and nostrils.

He slurred, "You come with me little varmint, you have a thing or two to learn."

He balanced his footing trying to carry her on his back. With one footstep he splashed into the creek almost dropping them both into the icy murky shallow edge. She felt terror, *"Oh no, we're going to fall in and freeze to death."*

"Put me down, I'm cold, and I'm not Sadie." Ann's heart was racing with panic.

Her heartbeat banged on her throat. She felt disoriented not knowing where he was taking her or what was happening. The scenery is flashing by in the dark like a scary movie where everything is blurred together. His breathing is becoming heavier struggling to keep her on his shoulder still. The jarring trip knocked the wind out of her preventing any attempts to scream.

He unlatched the hook to the chicken coop heaving to catch his breath. He reeked of beer now carrying Ann as if she were a baby inside. The coop was 16 by 20 feet in size. The rolled roof over the wood was glazed by frost. The wood burning stove released a smell of coal through the air piping out steam from the round metal chimney. There was a raggedy clean beige sheet dividing a small space in the back of the coop. A small white refrigerator was in the corner on top of the well swept lath floor. He stumbled over the sofa bed and pushed back the sheet curtain with force. He hurled her onto the bed.

"You can have Elsie's candy from the icebox if you let me play with you Annie."

She pursed her lips together and moved her head side to side as if rejecting bad medicine. "No, I don't wanna." Ann's eyes stung with tears and longed for someone to rescue her. As she fought more and more he got angry.

"Sadie loves me. Don't you?" He tries to guide her hand. "Put this in your mouth."

She rips her hand away, "No, I don't wanna." *"What's going on here?"*

The veins on his forehead were expanded. His grip on her small body left hand imprints. She is petrified and sobbing out of control. She breathed in and out short breaths like an instrument playing in staccato, "n-n-n-no," She yells with an earsplitting shriek.

*"I want my mommy, why is he doing this? It feels bad, it feels wrong. I'm scared."*

"Sadie, doesn't love you, nobody loves you." She flails her arms and legs to resist. The pot belly stove was releasing the odor of coal. Ann smelled the air and felt the force of her panicked breath in and out of her nose and mouth.

"Stop it Ann," He yells with an authoritative tone. "Stop fighting me. It will be better for you if you do it."

His devil eyes were bloodshot as a result of booze mixed with anger. He got louder with a crescendo of annoyance, "You better do as I say or you know what's good for you."

"No, no, no please stop, no." His breath reeked of alcohol and she tried backing away from him crying.

"Stop cryin', you need to stop bein' a baby."

She stood on the bed to try to escape but he pulled her back down. "You hafta learn."

"No I don't. I want my mommy, stop it," She yells back.

She tried crawling away by inching her knees nearer to the edge of the bed but he yanked her back close to him. He grabbed her head and tried pulling and shoving it down.

Her neck was hurting from resisting. She shook her head side to side and her hair slapped her face stinging each time. "No." The letter o resonated as she fought.

"Well if you're not gonna put it in your mouth, I want you to rub it."

"No. I'm not doing that either." When he tried to direct her, she kept pulling her hand away as if she were avoiding touching a searing stove.

He blinked his eyes to focus from seeing blurry. He covered Ann's mouth and whispered, "Wait here." He got up from the bed, walked over to his 22 rifle and patted it as if it needed reassurance. He gritted his teeth and with nostrils twitching from resentment, "Remember how I took care of that groundhog Ann? You better not tell. We'll try this again soon." He pulled his jeans back up. *Zip.*

He raised his hand to backhand her, "Stop crying." His incisors were in full view from his open mouthed scream.

Ann's head was jerking to one side sniffling as her shoulders rose and fell with each convulsing motion trying to stifle her whimper.

"I will *kill* you if you tell your mommy."

*"I'm supposed to be at grandmas."*

In her mind she wanted to run far away. In her body she was too small, overpowered and afraid to run. Her head spun in an astonishing fog thinking of how to escape the chicken coop.

# Chapter 2

# *Hurricane*

It's supper time. Elsie cooks beans, grits and corn bread again. They eat the same thing almost every day. She tastes the beans, "Yep, they're done, we can eat now." Elsie looks tired having given birth to John. She is functioning with little sleep and the sleeplessness has left her exhausted.

Sadie says, "Mama the baby is so beautiful." She scans his pint size body from top to bottom and side to side with marvel.

John is three days old and sleeping in a swaddled hand me down blanket. His tiny abdomen is expanding up and down as he breathes. He safe guards the sides of his head with small fists. She inhales the baby's aroma in a long slow breath and smiles, "I love the baby lotion and powder smell." John holds her finger with an automatic tug. She squeals, "Look, he's holding my finger, may I feed him?"

"You *may* go down to the river and rinse a diaper, that's what I need you for. Get excited about that."

Elsie yells out of the front door cupping one side of her mouth, "Esau get in here, foods done." Sadie gives her a puzzled look. "Well at least you'll have something to look forward to when you get older, *rinsing diapers.*"

"Okay mommy," Sadie writes off her crankiness as being tired and skips away. "I'll help Ann set the table."

Esau comes in sweating out alcohol with inflamed brown and red eyes from binge drinking the night before. His hair is slicked back with Brylcreem.

Elsie's eyes narrow, she's suspicious Esau took a long while returning home from work with extra cologne.

He runs his hands through his reddish brown hair and sings the old commercial, "A little dab will do ya, the girls they will pursue ya. They'll love to run their fingers through your hair." He laughs, "I'm a handsome fella aren't I? Take off my boots woman, my feet are aching."

Elsie squats down, looks up into his eyes, smiles and unties his boots. "You *are*. Where did you run off to when I was in the hospital?"

He avoids looking at her and clears the lump in his throat. He looks at Ann sitting at the table with eyes of warning. Elsie's head is down and he nods to the corner of the chicken coop where they live and looks over at Ann again. Elsie notices the strange nervousness of Ann's demeanor as a tinge of red covers the light freckles on her face. Elsie scrutinizes the menacing look on Esau's face but looks the other way.

Ann gulps looking at her father terrified, "*I better not tell he'll kill me like he said.*" She averts her eyes from everyone and puts her head down. "*What kinda father are you?*"

Esau clears the soft black wisps away from Elsie's cheek with his index finger, "Tuck those behind your ears, they make you look too nice. He pats her on the head, "I was just checking on the chicken coop is all." He stands up towering, all of 6'4," with a 220 pound formidable frame over Elsie's medium height and curvy body. Her exquisiteness brightened up a room.

Small speckles of black decorate Elsie's green eyes as she looks up at Esau. She smiles at him in adoration and follows him over to where the children are waiting.

Esau sits next to Annie and grabs her hand first and squeezes it, "Let's bless the food." Sadie notices, "*Oh no, is he going to hurt her too?*" He shoots a glare at Sadie and she bows her head and squeezes her eyes shut hoping it will make him go away.

He bows his head, "Lord, bless this food and all these children here. Let them grow up to love and praise you as I do Lord. We don't have much but one day we will God, with your strength. You always provide all our needs. We wanna keep servin' you with all our hearts. You will keep us from the sinfulness this world has to offer. You will be our Shepherd and we shall not want, Amen." Everyone chimes in, "Amen."

Elsie served everyone at the table and cradled John. Observing his mother Evan asks, "Why you always wait to eat last mama?"

George slaps Evan on the head, "cuz she wants to dummy."

Esau pounds his fists on the table making the plates, glasses and silverware rattle. "No talking during dinner. The veins on his neck are protruding. "No talking ever, unless I say," He yells. Maybe a hot belt would do you good." He grabs his belt buckle.

Elsie looks at them and back down to the baby. She remembers all the extreme beatings she received as a little girl and continues taking care of John. This was another normal evening for her. *"I guess things don't change just because you get married."*

He stands up in a rage and snarls, "Better than a belt, I think you boys look like you need some medicine." He pours a cup of hot water and mixes in a tad of turpentine. "Heard the neighbors saying this is healthy as castor oil. They say it tastes like heck though." He stirs with a scowl on his face. "I'll put a bit this time in case. When you boys get older I'll put the full two spoons."

"Here, George you drink first, you're *the mean one.*"

George's green eyes widen, "But that's poison daddy...you use that with paint."

He slaps George on the mouth, "I said shut up," He raises his voice. "This ain't poison; I heard it's healthy and good for you."

A tiny burst of blood leaks through the small crack on his lip. He licks the bitter copper taste of blood and raises his hand to drink the concoction. He bites his lip so the blood won't show. He doesn't want to give his father the satisfaction of being hurt. He feels

empowered he can't be weakened. *"I'll show him.*
George gulps with his eyes enlarged. *"Golly this
burns, ouch."*

Esau laughs, "You get healthy *and* learn a lesson.
How 'bout that?" He watches George's eyes water,
"Clears your sinuses don't it. Good for colds too."

George sits back down in silence. He puts his
palms on the table trying not to make any sudden
moves.

Esau prepares a cup for Evan. Evan's big brown
eyes look up with his head still bowed in reverent
fear. With hands trembling he drinks from the cup. He
coughs, gagging after drinking and grabs his throat.
He gives Esau the cup with a croaky tone, "Thank
you daddy."

"Stop kissing up and eat your food."

Esau sits and takes a bite, "Blasted food is cold
now." He mumbles as he chews his food. "Everyone
eat," Esau commands.

"I can heat that up for you if you want Esau,"
Elsie raises her voice from across the room. "Don't
take much."

Esau buries his face in his plate with a distant
look, "Don't bother, your kids ruined dinner."

One swirling hurricane blew into their home, hurricane Esau. He knew the passionate nuances of each
person in his trail. He stirred their feelings before they
knew he was approaching through manipulation and
control. If evil had an embodiment it would be Esau;
someone who appeared ordinary with a storm of
wickedness brewing within. The king of his domain

and the jester of his mind games, Esau had supper with his marionettes.

Elsie had a strong sense of her identity but surrendered her wholeness to him in return for crumbs of affection. She thought she was strong enough to endure but each moment whittled away at her. She busied herself in her world of denial hoping it would all change on its own.

The Oakridge Quartet is harmonizing "I'll fly away" in the background from an antique radio with one bent antenna.

*"Some glad mornin' when this life is o'er."* The bass singer sings his part, *"Bum, bum, bum."* They all sing in unison. *"I'll fly away."* The tenor sings, *"To a home where joy will never end,"* then the magic happens—they all harmonize, *"I'll fly away."*

Elsie hums along enjoying the harmony. She is watering her prized green plant with one hand and breast feeding with the other. She has rolled up jeans to keep cool which complimented Esau's flannel shirt she wore for the baby's easy access. "There ya go baby boy, you're hungry today." The baby is dozing off to sleep and suckles slower and slower. She sets him down for his nap bending her knees and covers him with the same blanket she used while feeding him. She stretches and yawns along with him.

With both hands she wrapped her long wavy black hair around one hand and positioned it on the back of her head. Her hair transformed into a French twist with bobby pins primed for housework and Esau's taste. *"God forbid. Esau would yell at me for lookin' nice with my hair down."*

After she watered the plant she starts reading her *True Story* magazine she hid from Esau. She reads her magazine, *"Hmm, the truth is stranger than fiction huh."* Making sure he wasn't watching her indulge in her guilty pleasure, Elsie looks over to see if there is any food left for her to eat.

Ann stares across the table to her mother Elsie. *"Don't you know? Can't you tell?"*

She glances at her father Esau when he's not looking. *"How can you act like you didn't do anything?"*

The radio continues to ring out, *"Just a few more weary days and then."* The baritone rumbles, *"Sweet Jesus,"* In harmony they all join in, *"I'll fly away; to a land where joy shall never end, I'll fly away,* they all slow down for the finale, *(I'll fly away)."* The bass singer ends with, "ay" and goes to the lowest note all gospel aficionados cherish as much as they applaud the highest pre-pubescent sounding note.

# Chapter 3

# *Remodeling*

A nn catches a glimpse of herself in a nearby full length mirror at the home she is remodeling. She jolts her head from the flashback and looks into her own green eyes through transparent protective glasses. *I'll fly away* trails off like a reverberated memory in her head. She is 54 now and taller than average with a body that shows years of physical labor. She's not heavy but well formed with short dirty blonde hair. Because it's unkempt from working, she flattens one side sticking up with a couple hard pats. *"I'm losing money on this job. It's taking longer than estimated."* She notices her client, Tina Louise walk into focus behind her reflection.

"I'll be out of your hair for the rest of the day." Tina is looking at Ann in the reflection.

Ann turns around. "Okay."

If you need help with this stiff wallpaper, call me. If it helps cut the cost, I'll do what it takes Ann."

"Okay," Ann repeats in a calm tone.

Tina reassures Ann she is willing to lend a hand knowing she was the one who over glued the wallpaper in the first place. She puts her hand on her chin in thought, *"I knew I put too much of that glue. It never curled up or bubbled though."* "Don't be shy I'm willing to help."

Ann looks down from the ladder and in her reserved soft monotone voice says, "Okay, I'll do what I can. I'll be here a while looks like."

Tina is wearing a neon green track suit and white golf hat. Although her track suits never saw a track or a gym and her hat a golf course, she appeared athletic. All through winter and spring her suits changed colors along with a variety of muscle shirts underneath. When cold in the morning and warmer in the afternoon, she wore her short pants they called knickers in her day. They went in and out of style and when they renamed them *Capri*, she kept the same pants but changed the name. Because of the unpredictable weather of the Midwest, this day she had on her Capri pants with a track suit jacket. She fanned herself. "Whew, glad I wore my *Capri* pants today; all I have to do is take off this jacket and I'm ready for this tropical climate." She looks down at her pants, "Serious, these things never go out of style, you watch, after this year of 2010, they'll always be around."

Ann smiles with a cordial grin and says, "I tried leaving the window open for airing. The temperature in here feels comfortable for working." Ann continues focusing on her work yet looking at her client when she can.

Tina grabs her keys from her matching fanny pack and zips it back up. She adjusts her hat, "I like these, they give you that cool feeling on the top of your head and keep the sweat from stinging your eyes. No wonder athletes wear them." She scratches her three inch high eighties poof crowning her cap with her pinky finger and she doesn't flatten it. The room exudes a grape smelling hairspray. She has the television remote control in her hand and aims towards it, "I don't know why my grandkids have to have it blaring all the time...they always leave it on."

Hannah Montana is singing, "You get the best of both worlds." *Click.*

She smiles and looks down at the remote with cookie crumbs in it and grins. "Sometimes I look out the window and the rear car doors are still open," She laughs, "They're precious though. Never dreamed I'd let them get away with so much."

Ann smiles at her.

"Call if you need me. I need to keep the expenses down, I have lots of bills...you know with the economy and all." She shakes her head with disapproval, "Tsk, tsk, how 'bout them gas prices." She wiggles her fingers, "Toodle-oo." She walks out of the room and leaves a lingering scent of hairspray.

Ann is struggling with the wallpaper, "Okay, bye." She tears off some small pieces, *"I have expenses too."* She takes her gloves off from the heat they cause and is aggravated she can't get some of the sections. Her mind wanders off again but her surroundings keep bringing her back.

Tina peers in the partially open window, "Oh, and Bam-Bam will *meow* for attention, you can ignore her. She'll let herself in an out of the automatic pet door. I'll be back."

Emotionless Ann says, "Okay." She enjoyed conversation but was focused while working. Some may have thought she lacked expression but years of abuse formed her personality. She had a notion she would have to expand her words someday to a genre of women with the same history. She struggled with this concept all her life until she couldn't battle it anymore. Along with her insurmountable work, she believed she had to relate her story because she was haunted by the isolation her secret caused.

A mangy grey cat like the one resurrected in a movie growled in the background. It looked more like a wild tom cat than a domesticated female feline. It bellowed a wicked sounding snarl, "mee-ow-uh. Gurr."

Ann is crying and looks at the cat. *"Oh shut up."* She continues thinking back to her original recollection, *"I didn't want you to do any of that to me."* She is frustrated because the wallpaper is not coming off easier. *"I sure as heck didn't want to do all that to you either, you pervert."*

The cat is staring at her with its pools of black dilated eyes swimming in grey, "Meow." It sees Ann's indifference and starts licking its paw and cleaning its ear.

Ann wipes tiny pieces of wallpaper from her paint crusted jeans and T-shirt. She wipes off more from her old tennis shoes as she goes down a few steps from the ladder to dispose of the debris she's collecting in her hands. She sprays hot water from a bottle and thumps the wall with a rag. "Who glued this stupid stuff on here? She ascends a few steps in a frustrated hurry to finish.

"Meow." The cat speeds away as if alarmed by something. It leaps out at full tilt as if it were a cheetah sprinting out of the automatic pet door. It makes a loud sound when exiting, "Bam."

Ann picks at the wallpaper with a trowel and careful handiness. She looks back at the wall and takes a shallow breath. She has removed the larger pieces but it's the small rigid ones she's working on. She prides herself in the skillful way she preserves the wall. "Good, don't wanna take any of the drywall off with this stubborn glue. I can always patch these up with plaster before I prime and paint." She feels a nagging tension in her neck.

She leans her head towards the ceiling and closes her eyes. *"I don't wanna hurt my family. Maybe it'll bring us closer together. No one wants to hear these gross stories. I told my closest friends, but what if I told the world? Would it help them?"* She opens her eyes again and looks at the clock; she's an hour behind now.

She hears the neighbor lady, "You may play outside but dinner will be ready soon."

Ann pounds her fist on the ladder. "C'mon wallpaper, we have a deadline," She raised her voice and looked around to make sure no one was there. She hits the trowel's edge, her right hand throbs with pain. *"Oops, ouch, I should be wearing gloves but this stuff is on here good."* Ann looks down, "I think what I need is more paper stripper." She looks in the long mirror, *"This isn't about the wallpaper is it?"*

"Alright mom," the children answer outdoors.

Ann's left hand comforts the hurt one. *"Now what?"* She sighs with a deep breath after holding it, able to catch it after chasing it for years. *"What if I don't rule it out?"*

Her phone rings but her hands are sullied with sticky paper strips. She hears her phone vibrating and sees it hopping around, *buzz buzz...buzz buzz...buzz buzz...buzz buzz.*

"If it's important they'll leave a message." Her shoulders relax; she rubs her neck until it unwinds and rolls her head around. Large tears of anger turn to small streaks of resolve. Two separate lines mark a trail on her dusty face. She uses them to moisten the rest of her face with her rolled up jacket. The wall had wooden trim all around the room. It wasn't primed and Ann had to spray the entire room with orange peel.

"No, you're it." The neighbor children bellow.

She knows redemption is on the horizon, she doesn't know where or when it will arrive. She recognizes there is a reason the memories keep flooding back all at once. She wants to pay attention to the silent whisper destiny is beckoning in her spirit's ear.

Birds are chirping. She hears the children again, "C'mere Bam-Bam."

She looks out the taped window ready for new finishing. She has it cracked opened for adequate ventilation and decides she doesn't want to be upset anymore.

"That's enough crying for one day." She looks over at her phone blinking with a voicemail message. She sits at the third step of the ladder, wraps her arm around it as if it was a swing and retrieves her one message.

"Hi, we have a mutual friend who says you have a compelling story and you are interested in a book. It can help a lot of people. You know me as a recording artist but I'm an author also. I think I can help tell your story because I've been through some things myself. Please call back at this number. My name is..."

Ann's mind trails off remembering a motivational speaker, "If you've ever experienced abuse on any level, it's embarrassing but given a voice, it speaks to save your life."

Her memories start zooming in and out now. They are ablaze in her mind and in a vivid flash she sees her young self in a car making a promise.

*"I'm sure I'm not the only one who's been through this. If writing this book can help one less child get abused. Boy that boils my blood. If it can help one adult deal with his or her pain, it'd be worth it.*

Tears stream down her face again, *"When I see people trapped in their pain as adults I can't help but feel for them, poor mom. Man, if my story will give an abused wife courage to get help..."*

She puts the phone back where it was, still thinking.

*"I made a promise years ago. I think it's time. I'm gonna give my story and voice, I'm gonna save lives."*

She continues to work alone. "Mom only shot that gun trying to protect us. Hmm, why did the neighbor think he was welcomed in our house?" She says to herself, *"Oh yeah, now I remember."*

# Chapter 4

# *Love thy neighbor*

I t's near springtime and Jephod Ankleman, one of Esau Flink's neighbors knocks on the door giving the hook a clatter. While waiting for an answer, he takes the orange rag from his back pocket and wipes his sweaty brow. From left to right he wipes over his forehead feeling the scar on his left eye, reminded of the truck that once fell on him.

He could have walked to the Flink's home but he had fishing gear he wanted to show Esau. His stereo is turned on and Bluegrass, his favorite music, is playing in the background. Standing at the door, his 8-track tape was finishing up the last chorus before it started over.

*Oh, the hills, beautiful hills, How I love those West Virginia hills*
*If o'er sea o'er land I roam, Still I'll think of happy home,*
*And my friends among the West Virginia hills.*

He is wearing dark blue overalls with hints of dark stains from car grease. His thick black hair is slicked back with pomade. He's pudgy and short yet he thinks dark colors make him look taller and slimmer. He looks down at his leather shoes. He has sky blue eyes, which is his best feature. He smiles knowing his shoes would dress up his overalls. Setting the crawfish cage down; he gives the door a jangle after knocking on it again. He strains to steal a look inside through the cracks on the front door moving his head up and down, side to side. He's singing in a soft tone, *"I'm the one who loves you."*

Elsie walks towards the door, she hears the baby scream.

Jephod is trying to catch a glimpse of her through the door cracks. It was warmer now and Elsie had removed the old rags she used to cover the cracks. His heart starts to race. *"She is so beautiful with those green eyes and that beautiful body."*

The baby is crying with a piercing howl and she turns around again. "Be right there, gonna see about the baby," She calls over her shoulder.

She bends over to check on John. *"What do you want this time, I haven't slept for days. I'm tired."* John is turning dark pink shaking with fury. *"What is wrong with you, I fed you and changed you."*

Jephod is in a trance remembering peeping at Elsie while she worked on the clothes line. *"She knows how to work a line. The way she picks each clothes pin off hand over hand like a classical pianist."* Elsie is unaware she is being watched. *Humming she bends over to put clothes in the straw basket. "Yes, she looks like that naked centerfold in my wallet." He pulls out his wallet and compares Elsie to the centerfold. "Elsie, I'm in love with you in my mind. You need to see it in my actions. If I come around enough you'll love me like I love you...besides, I can take better care of you than Esau. He looks at her with a burning lust, "Or I can just take you." Elsie feels someone is looking at her and turns around to check. Jephod fumbles back behind a large oak tree and drops the ripped out magazine centerfold and wallet.*

*Elsie calls out, "Who's there?" Jephod waits until he hears humming again and peeks around.*

*He looks at her while picking up his wallet and picture. "Wow, I love how the sun is showing her sexy silhouette."*

While still in his imagination Jephod is singing. Elsie walks towards the door again with a flowered form fitted house dress on. Her bare feet slap the wood floor with each step headed towards the door. She finishes buttoning the top button of her dress knowing an unexpected guest is at the door. "What do you want Jephod? That you singin' out there?"

He looks at her dress and envisions unbuttoning it from top to bottom and having his way with her. Elsie snaps her fingers at the screen door above her head, "Jephod?"

Jephod stares.

"Hmm, I didn't know you could sing; sounds okay I guess."

"Ahem." Swallowing hard he looks past her, "I was wondering if Esau wanted to go craw fishing again.

"Wait out here I'll get Esau."

*"She likes me."* He smiles and picks up the cage again. It was no secret; Jephod Ankleman was in lust with Elsie Flink. In his delusion he thought it was love. He gave a whole new meaning to *love thy neighbor.*

Esau walks up and doesn't like the way Jephod is looking at Elsie. With an angry tone he barks, "What you want Jephod?"

"Let's go craw fishing again Esau; gotta trap I made from left over wire. I have firewood back home to cook them and beer to wash 'em down." Jephod is gazing at Elsie, "Maybe Elsie can come along."

Sadie and Ann both run up to Elsie to tell her the baby is crying and needs his diaper changed again.

Jephod looks at the girls from top to bottom. *"She has very pretty girls. They're going to be beautiful like their mama."* "Your girls are real pretty Elsie."

Esau with creased brows puts his hand on Elsie's back to guide her away, "Elsie and the girls have to take care of the baby. I already promised Evan and George we'd catch fish by ourselves. I learned an old Indian trick the other day. I brought coal from the mine at work. Won't be needin' that trap, won't be needin' you neither."

Jephod holds his trap close to his chest with a big goofy smile. He takes another long lustful gawk at Elsie as she's moving in the background, "Alright, maybe another time." He turns around and his smile transforms into sulk and walks away.

"I don't like the way he looks at you; like he's undressin' you with his eyes Elsie."

"It's no different from how you look at other women Esau."

He slaps her arm real hard leaving a welted red hand print, "See that print right there? That mark on you says you're mine."

Elsie's eyes water with coldness, "You should go with the boys before it gets dark."

Looking pale and tired Elsie shuffles her feet towards the baby again, *"I still have to wash diapers and make supper for the rest of the children. I don't know how much more I can take."*

Esau picks up the pail they used to fill the large tub for bathing. "We'll use this to boil the crawfish. I'll take some pans too."

Esau looks at Evan and George, "You boys ready to do some fishin'?"

"Can we get some milk on the way back daddy, we're out." George is looking in the small fridge. He pulls out the carton and turns it upside down shaking the few drops left.

"Can't afford it, drink water. Let's go."

George stomps off, *"Yeah but you can afford your beer."*

Evan is dressed in his old donated clothes. He has broad shoulders and skinny legs and is starting to look like Esau.

George fussing with his pants looks to Evan and says, "Pretty soon I'll hafta borrow your pants. I'm out growing mine."

Esau laughs, "The way George eats, that big ole boy won't be wearin' Mr. Skinny Leg's clothes.

George tones down the sarcastic reply in his head remembering his split lip, "Well bein' hungry makes me the best at catching crawfish, I poke them with a stick and let them grab on."

Evan rolls his eyes, "I'll get the poles, bucket and fishin' box." Evan whispers to George as he walks past him. "Fatty."

George makes sure Esau isn't looking and sticks his tongue out from his plump cheeks.

Esau looks at Ann and Sadie, "You girls want to come along?"

Ann and Sadie grab each other's hands and in a unanimous voice say, "No."

Esau looks at the youngest boys Joseph and Butch napping on the bed, "Suit yourselves, c'mon Evan and George, let's go fishing."

Esau, Evan and George make their way towards the creek. Signs of spring are beginning in Wolford. As they approach, the flat large rocks are high above the creek and look imposing as the falls roll into the river. It is alive with frogs diving around the edges and fish swarming in patches of waters. Its bed is rippling down a long flowing infinite trail.

George runs straight to the creek. "Watch me catch craws with my hands," He yells. He crouches down and with his chubby fingers, he breaks off a twig from a fallen tree. He spots a crawfish and begins to poke it.

Evan comes in closer to watch and puts his hand on George's shoulder, "Don't kill it, nudge it dimwit."

George slaps his hand away, "Get your own crawfish, dummy."

Esau walks up, "You boys settle down or there's some turpentine waiting for you at home."

Evan points to George, "He's poking it daddy."

Esau laughs, "George is always poking it."

"Poking what daddy?"

Shaking his head he thinks it's the best joke ever, "Never mind George, get to fishing I'm going to prepare the mud we'll use to cook the fish."

George yelps, "Ah-ow." It snapped me but I got one daddy." The crawfish is dangling from George's fingers desperate to escape. George's smile reveals a gap of two missing teeth he lost within four days. He puts it in the bucket and crunches down to catch another.

Esau smiles and nods at George.

Evan gets the fishing pole ready and hooks a cricket he picked up on the way to the creek. *"I'll catch one and make daddy proud."*

"Now you boys keep catching, I'll build the fire." Esau builds a fire with coals he brought in a large potato bag. He places two Y shaped twigs at both edges of the fire and pulls a twig through the pale handle he filled with water. "Bring those craws over George; I'm fixin' to boil them."

Esau walks over to the edge of the creek and starts getting a huge fistful of mud.

George hops over to Esau with the crawfish he caught. "What you gonna do with that mud daddy?"

"I'm goin' to make you each eat these two thick mud pies I'm makin'."

Evan and George both hold their breath and look at each other with dread.

Esau is amused by their reaction and throws his head back, "Naw, I'm gonna put the fish between these here patties and cook 'em in the coals. That's how the Indian's used to do it."

Evan and George laugh with nervousness making sure to let their overbearing father know he is funny.

"That's funny daddy. Oh," He yells. I felt a tug he's a good size fish."

"Okay Evan you gotta be careful to reel him in slow, you can lose him. That bobber jerked under real good."

"Boy, I can really feel him fightin' daddy."

"Alright, tug a little more; you'll hook it real good in his mouth. Now draw your pole back and reel him in slow."

"He's comin', c'mon dinner, come to papa," Evan laughs.

"He's gettin' tired; you can probably finish pullin' him in. Lemme get you the gloves so he's not slippery."

"That's okay dad I'll use these pliers. Yeah, look at him; he's a real beauty daddy."

"Bring him over Evan. He's about a 10 or 12 lb. large mouth, good size."

Evan is glowing with satisfaction after receiving the first near compliment from his father he has ever heard. *"He likes my fish."*

George yells, "Got another one. He ain't as big as the others but he'll eat."

Evan picks the first finished crawfish out of the pail with a stick. "You pull the back part and there's the meat. Esau hisses, "It's steamy but looks good."

He sucks the head making loud slurping noises. Esau eats the first one. He always eats first, no exceptions.

He blows on the crawfish before he eats it, "This first one's mine, you boys can have the next ones. Yeah, these are good...better than lobster." Although he's never eaten lobster, he likes to make himself more significant.

The sun is starting to set as Esau picks at the dried mud patties that turned to cooked clay. The fire made a crackling sound and spat out embers. He turns over the contraption he keeps by the creek near a red mulberry tree he uses to cook fish. There are six impaled fish all lined up head to fishtail. The large object looked like a giant fork with thinner wires and a handle. "Come on over boys and watch how the clay cooked this fish."

He peels back the top layer of the clay. "When the eye is white it's done cookin'. You grab the skeleton and pull it right out."

"How does the fish not get dirty with mud?" Evan looks disgusted.

Esau reaches in, "The skin touches the clay but the insides are steamed cooked and come out easy and tender."

"That's neat dad can I have more crawfish?" George looks in the pan.

"Yeah, I cooked some leaves that turned to salt, you add that."

This black stuff, looks like gun powder? Evan points at the powder in a pan.

"Yep, that'll give it flavor." Esau pulls out the guitar case and opens it up. He begins to strum some songs to soothe himself. He looks distant and preoccupied about something. It was as if the guitar playing triggered a thought.

Evan stares at his father a moment. *"I wish he was like this all the time."*

"It's gonna get dark soon; we're going to have to get back." Esau looks at his watch. He looks to the sky and notices the bottom of the sun is dipping into the horizon. He was reminded of Darla as he looks at the different colors the sunset radiated. The blend of orange, yellow, rust, brown and a dash of white are exploding from the sunset's announcement of the day's end. *"Darla's husband should be going into work about now. I oughta pay her a visit. I haven't had a drink all day, I'm thirsty too."*

# Chapter 5

# *Romanticize*

D arla is almost finished sowing her dress. *"Ah yes, it's the latest fashion with a touch of the roaring 20's."*

*Don't wake me up let me dream,* was the 20's song playing on her beautiful vintage wooden phonograph record player. The album had an old style buzz making it sound like the orchestra was playing through a phonograph cylinder. *"Daddy loved this music."*

The phone rings, "Hello? Oh hi honey. Uh-uh. Oh you're going to work at the mine till morning? Be careful. I haven't seen you in days since you've been working two jobs. It's been hard on us. Okay, see you in the morning. Bye." She hangs up the phone and looks around the room with a lonesome longing.

Her home was decorated with a romantic feel. Darla had a comfortable style appealing to the senses through soft fabrics, floral patterns, lace, painted furniture, and a pastel colored palette. She loved everything soft like the light that filtered through the sheer curtains. She refused to use artificial flowers and preferred aromatic flower arrangements.

On her dark wooden coffee table she had a pearl shell and a silver vase with one framed family photo of her and her husband. Beside it was a copy of the novel "Pride and Prejudice" sitting next to it.

Darla smiles and looks over at the picture of her parents on the table she worked. Although they divorced and went their separate ways, memories of her lavish upbringing lived on in her mind. Her new dress reminded her of her first visit with her dad in New York after the divorce. She could afford to buy almost any dress but nothing suited her style.

Admiring her new dress she looks at the clock, *"I wonder if Esau will come over again, he's so kind and generous."*

She put on her pastel colored dress. It was a light teal green with white flowers on it. The built in belt had an embroidered flower on the left side down at her hip. She was proud of the lowered waistline at her hips. The sheer sleeves were light teal. The remaining 8" of the flared hem reached to mid-thigh because of her long regal legs. She was used to slouching because her husband was much shorter, *"Now I top it off with the floral perfume Esau bought me. I love this dress, I did well."*

Her stunning blonde hair was up with an elegant twist and a rhinestone accented hair comb. The teal color made her blue eyes seem clear. She rubbed scented cream into her ivory colored skin. She kicked up her matching shoes, "He's going to love this look."

The doorbell rang and Darla, giddy with excitement claps her hands together as if she won a prize. She opens the door with a huge pining smile and wraps her arms around Esau's neck as she takes in his scent of hair cream and cologne, "I love to stand up tall when I'm with you."

She kisses him on the cheek and on the lips. "I'm surprised you didn't let yourself in like you always do." She laughs, "I always find you sitting here on my couch..." She gestures with her hands, "...like a sneaky slithery snake."

"Well I would but my hands are full. I'm trying' to catch you in a towel or even less."

She kisses him again.

He steps back and looks around. "We're still outside Darla."

Crickets were in the background as evening started to set in.

"Don't be silly Esau, it's almost dark out and no one is around."

Esau is standing at the doorway with a six pack of beer in a brown bag and a store baked specialty pie for Darla.

"Thanks for the pie; it's thoughtful of you." She takes the pie as if it's an expensive bottle of fine wine.

Esau looks around and closes the door behind him.

Jephod Ankleman was watching for Esau to leave his chicken coop home to sneak a look at Elsie. This time he decided to follow Esau to see what he was up to. *"I knew it. I gotta go tell Elsie. For sure she'll leave him and be with me."*

Esau sat on the couch, "Can you please put these in the fridge, leave some out will ya. I'm thirsty."

"Are you going to play the banjo for me today Esau?"

"Can't believe you bought me one Darla," he chuckles. *"That was nice."*

She bats her false lashes with a flutter, "Well you're always kind to me." She walks over and hands Esau the banjo and sits next to him. *"I should tell him the banjo story; he'll feel smart for playing one."*

She clasps her hands together and faces him on the couch. "Did you know banjos came from an Arabian instrument, and went to Africa, and America? I learned that in private school."

"Well aren't you the smart one, look at you." *Nothin' like that kinda information to make me feel stupid."*

"Why don't you go to the kitchen and I'll play while you put the pie away," He lusts after her long legs watching them stride towards the kitchen while he plays.

She yells from the kitchen, "Esau, you want me to cut you a piece of pie?" She checks her purse to make sure she took her birth control pill. *"I hope tonight is our first night."* Upper middle class and wealthy people could afford those pills.

"Pie and beer don't go together; you can save it if you want." He chugs down the first beer with a few swigs. He picks up the novel from the coffee table. "Pride and Prejudice, hmm, I can't believe you read this crap."

He looks at her husband's picture. *"What a loser, he can't keep his woman satisfied."*

Darla walks back in and giggles, "Romance is my way of escape, I'm always here alone."

After chugging down his second beer he looks at Darla, "Run away with me, I'll help you escape."

"Oh Esau, can we move to New York?"

"Of course, c'mere." *"You look pretty."* He removes the comb from her hair. *"I love your hair down, turns me on. I like your dress."* He wraps his hands around her back still facing her. "Let me help you with that dress."

Darla stops Esau's hand, "Only if you leave Elsie. I can't give myself to you without a commitment. I'm not that kind of girl."

He smiles, *"Sure you're not."* He smells her neck, "You're wearing that perfume I bought you." *"Smells nice,"* he thinks to himself.

"I am. Your gifts are all thoughtful."

She pulls back still in his embrace, "Why don't we ever go see a movie or something, it's dark enough in there. No one will know."

"Movies are sinful don't ya know Darla?"

He drinks more and sets the tin can on the embroidered coaster of the coffee table. "I'll do anything you want me to Darla."

Jephod is looking at their outlines through the window as they kiss and begin to undress each other. *"That's it. Elsie is mine, now."*

He runs down the road as fast as he can. *"Soon as I tell Elsie she'll be so angry with Esau she'll be with me."*

A few amiable gestures, a smile in passing, and an affirming nod, were all the things in a woman Jephod Ankleman needed to make his move. Now with a philandering husband, Jephod scored. He was confident in his daydream she would run away with him, and for all these things he presumed justification. In his utopia women as striking as Elsie were in abundance...but the women in his reality were homely and unattended. Elsie's natural magnificence was worth the chase. Lust had engrossed him, and obscured by it, he ran to claim what was his in his mind.

Out of breath from running over a mile he reaches the chicken coop. He pounds on the door. "Elsie, open the door." Jephod pounds on the door harder. "Open up," Jephod insists. He pulls on the door and tries to unlatch the hook from the eye. He starts to rattle it and she sees the tips of his fingers. He wiggles them through the crack of the door. Esau always made her lock the door when he left because of his paranoia. This time it wasn't mere paranoia menacing his family.

Elsie hears a male voice who isn't Esau. She runs to the corner of the chicken coop and grabs the 22 rifle. The children are all terrified and begin to cry. "You better get away from the door, I gotta gun."

"Elsie, open c'mon."

Cold sweat crawls down her spine. The primal desire to protect her family sets in. "Kids go hide behind the couch." She has an inclination to faint as her knees buckle. Shaking her head to gain composure, she raises the gun. She widens her eyes to regain focus. The room stops spinning.

She hears the door rattle as Jephod tries to jingle the hook loose from the hole again. She shoots her rifle above the door with a mindless reflex. *Ping.* The gunshot makes a clean sound as it punches another hole in the chicken coop. Esau in many of his drunken rages would fire the gun. Their home was adorned with bullet holes courtesy of Esau. Elsie felt comfortable adding yet another. The smell from the gunfire afterward was lingering. The children all scream at once. "You're scarin' my kids, go away," Elsie says with a loud, shaky tone.

Jephod yells, "I saw Esau kissing Darla and they were doing things. Let's be together, we can get back at him." He lowers his voice in a more angry tone. "Open this door right now Elsie or I'll just take you without your permission," He persists.

"I missed on purpose before." Elsie raises her voice and her pitch gets louder and higher as she goes up on her tipped toes, "It won't happen again."

"Aw, c'mon Elsie, you can do better than Esau, he's with someone else right now, don't you see he don't want you like I do."

The voice behind the door sounded familiar but Elsie was scared and didn't stop to figure it out.

"I said go *away.* Who do you think you are? What makes you think you gotta right to be with me? I'm going to tell my husband."

She cocks the gun again and she hears him run away.

# Chapter 6

# *Withholding*

They had their first tryst together. They are both sweaty and out of breath. Darla smiles and rolls over on her side, props herself on her elbow and outlines Esau's chest. Her own is exposed to him. *"You were withholding all these times."* "I know you ignore me because you're busy and not because you don't love me Esau." She stares into his eyes, "I'm glad I gave myself to you tonight. *I hope you never stop loving me. I'm falling hard for you."*

He looks at her and looks away. "Don't you feel bad for what we just did Darla?"

"Well no Esau, I love you. We're going to run away together."

Darla is making little circles around Esau's chest with her finger.

"I could never leave Elsie for you."

Esau never told her he loved her. He scarcely paid her compliments. He showered her with gifts because he knew how materialistic she was. In her eyes the gifts were just as good as being loved. It was an equal trade. His pay off was his benevolent image which earned him approval. Her reward was receiving gifts replacing love. She was accustomed to inheriting presents from her guilt ridden parents, her father in particular.

The album is hissing in the background and the singer sings, *Boo, boo, bee, doo.*

She convinced herself after many years love came in a box delivered to her house with a card reading, "To my beautiful angel; a gift from your daddy."

Although Esau was the one giving effects, her flattery was like a drug to him. After giving to a great extent he would ignore her and draw away and watch her chase after him calculatingly. He knew the manipulation would get her into bed at some point. After the seduction and getting what he wanted, the thrill of the chase would diminish. He would go on the prowl, hunting another needy, vulnerable victim and pick his target.

Darla is stunned Esau has broken his promise to be with her and sits up. She pulls the covers over herself with an indignant look and is now feeling shame for being naked. *"This can't be happening."*

"You promised me Esau, you promised we'd run away together."

Esau gets up from the bed and puts his clothes on. "I need more beer, I gotta go."

Darla feels her face getting hot. Her heart is pumping harder than she has ever felt. She has a queasy feeling in her stomach and her chest tightens with resentment. Tears of anger burst from her eyes,

"Now you grow a conscience? You lie to me and use me?"

"I'll come back tomorrow and we can do it again if you want Darla. I like you but you're not a virgin."

"What the h…" She motions towards the door and stomps her foot, anger taking control of her body. "Get out. Get out *now*." She yells, "I never want to see you ever again you monster." She picks up his shoes and throws them at him, "Don't ever come back here you stupid *hill billy*."

"You're the tramp who gave it up easy. You think you Nazarene's are better and holier?" He yells with disgust as his upper lip is raised with a sneer. He looks at her up and down as if she were putrid garbage. "You're white trash, you ain't no *high class*. Look at you."

"No, look at you," Her lips are quivering as she yells, "I'll tell Elsie."

She steps towards him and takes a swing at Esau. He grabs her arm midway, "She won't believe you anyway."

Darla grits her teeth, and points towards the door again, "Get out." She shakes her head with fury and her hair becomes tousled, "Leave," she stomps and continues bawling, "I thought I was in love with you, I gave myself to you." She pulls her sheet up higher.

Esau takes a rueful gasp, "Look maybe we can work things out. We'll stay with our spouses but have a *fling*. Let's talk about this."

"Leave," She yells. Darla pushes him out of her room throws his shoes on the living room floor, shuts and locks the door bemoaning. She's standing with her back against the door with a posh high thread count sheet draped around her body. Her hands are on her face and she is sobbing with guilt and remorse. She doubles over feeling the physical pain of abandon. She slides down the door until she's sitting and leans on an antique chair. As she romanticized about her childhood, she idealized Esau. The ache of losing what she had created in her mind was overwhelming.

Esau's eyes begin to water with regret as he puts on his shoes. *"I really did love you."*

He gets up to walk he hesitates wanting to talk Darla out of hating him but hears her sobbing. He knows he won't be able to sweet talk her again. He spins around and decides to leave, *"She's crying louder and louder. She's over me."*

The music is still playing in the background. *You're my sweet love, my sugar dove.*

He storms out the front door his steps straight, his mind staggering and makes it to the market for more beer. *"If it wasn't for that cow at home I could be with Darla."*

A great horned owl gave a deep booming hoot. It called, "hoo-hoo, hoo-hoo," and was heard over several miles during the still darkness.

Esau tucks a twelve pack under his arm while he opens and chugs another beer. *"But no, instead I have to go home to all those kids which probably aren't all mine."* Stopping at a nearby tree he slumps down drinking more beer. His head is beyond buzzing. Prickly sensations of the alcohol are radiating through his head. *"I lost you forever Darla."* He wipes his eyes with his thumb.

The owl gives a growling *kroo-oo* attacking his unsuspecting dinner. The call was eerie.

Slurring he yells, "I shoulda married a virgin." He tilts his head back to get each single drop and opens another can. He lost count now and attempts to get up. He trips and falls but feels nothing from being numbed by the alcohol. *"Shoot."* Quickly he tries to pick up the can he dropped before he loses what's left. *"Devil's workin' overtime today."*

A large American toad calls out with an elevated pitched shrill. The sound was fast and emulated a flute playing a high note. The night was alive though Esau notices none of it.

Esau gets up and staggers the rest of the way home. He stumbles through the door with an incoherent declaration, "I'm the man of the houth-th. I know what needstuh be. It's my life and whatever is left I say what I want to do right now like the Bible." He continues his rant quoting scriptures sprinkled with cuss words.

Elsie is furious, "Some man was just here tryin' to open the door. He kept yelling and saying you were down the road messin' with Darla Jones."

Esau slaps Elsie, "You slut," He slapped her hard and lost his balance. Trying not to fall he yells, "You were with Jephod-th Agg-ehl-man. I saw him peekin' behind a tree. First I thought he was followin' me to tell you. He was waitin' for me to be gone so he could mess around with you. That's it ain't it." He raises his arms and his voice, "Ain't it."

Elsie feels the tingle on her face as she touches it and leans into him. "So he's right, you were with her?" Elsie beats Esau's arm and pushes him. "You can't help but be with one floozy after another. There are lots of rumors about you." She takes a whiff, "You smell like beer again."

He becomes riled. He sobers for a moment from indignation. He taps her forehead with every syllable, "Don't you turn this around and make it about me Elsie; you know you're makin' up lies to cover up what you did."

Evan is resentful of the way Esau is turning everything around, "This isn't her fault. You stop talkin' to her like that. He expands his chest at Esau with his hands in tight balls. "Don't hit her again." He yells, "Hear me?"

Esau looks at Evan and at Elsie with more outrage. He kicks a chair and pounds on the wall. The chair screeches across the floor before toppling over. She can see his neck pulsating with fury.

Elsie looks at Esau in horror. *"Oh God help me, when he starts talking normal again after being so drunk he 'bout near kills me."*

"You owe an explanation, why do you keep actin' like this?" Evan tries to corner Esau. "Why you gettin' drunk so much? What are you hiding?"

With eyes like a rampant bull, Esau puts his head down and spots his aim. He pulls back and gives a hard blow to Elsie's stomach. She grunts and falls to the ground curled up not able to breathe. A piercing pain shoots down from her right shoulder. She feels her stomach begin to cramp. He kicks her in the stomach again for good measure. She feels her belly button burning. Her ears are ringing as she looks up.

The children are in a blur and some are waving their little hands motioning their father to stop.

Some of the children are in a huddle trying to console each other. Others are yelling, "No daddy stop, stop. Please daddy stop." Screaming and afraid for their mother they try to run towards her but the older ones are scared they'll get caught in the crossfire and hold them back.

Evan yells, "We can't let him do this." His hands are shaking and his lip is quivering. *"He's going to kill our mommy."*

Evan lunges at Esau, "This ends now." He misses Esau and is crying with resentment instead of fear.

Esau wobbles towards the bed, "Back off."

"Why do you keep actin' like this, when are you ever gonna stop." Evan is puzzled and trying to reason with his father. "What did she do that you're always so mad at her? It was that guy's fault tryin' to break in and take mom."

Esau sways seeing Evan double and bats his hand with a dismissive swat. Esau ignores Evan and staggers to the bed mumbling. He scrunches his face as if he smelled something rotten and with all the hatred he can collect he says, "I hope you lose that baby." As he falls on the bed he bounces as it squeaks in protest.

He buries the side of his head into the pillow, "It's probably not mine." He blacks out. Slobber pours out of the side of his mouth.

Evan runs to Elsie terrified, "Can I help you mommy?"

"Leave me alone Evan. You-ins make your father mad and he takes it out on me. I don't need your help."

Elsie is lying on the floor and within minutes the warmth of blood begins seeping out and down onto her legs. She can't move.

# Chapter 7

## *Sisters*

**"I** wish you'd just leave that man, Elsie. Do you sleep? The better question is...do you rest?"

"No, I ain't slept hardly in days, prolly weeks. I can't keep up."

"You look tired, you need to cut him off and leave him. He's a taker and you're a giver. He's an emotional vampire, Elsie. He'll suck you dry. Divorce him."

Elsie takes in a calming breath, smells potpourri and says," Hmm I know, Jackie, but God hates divorce."

Jackie faces Elsie on her colorful brown, orange and gold, clean lined sofa. "You know what God hates, Elsie?"

Elsie is barefoot and pinches the shag rug between her toes and looks up into Jackie's hazel eyes. "What?"

Jackie's home is neat and uncluttered. She decorated it in bold geometric shapes with wall hangings and curtains. She had area Moroccan rugs in assorted colors on her linoleum no-wax vinyl floor. There is a hutch with three antique dolls on stands a few shelves below her China. Even though she mimicked the popular television shows home décor, she was a realist and wasn't afraid to speak her mind. Her sense of style exuded her daring personality.

Jackie takes a long breath as if she were ready to give a speech. She punches a gold colored laced throw pillow each time she makes a statement, "Wanna know what God hates? God *hates* when Esau beats on you, He *hates* when Esau beats on the kids, He *hates* that Esau kicked you so hard he made you lose your baby…I mean it's…it's…downright murder." Jackie shakes her head.

Elsie makes a sighing sound.

Jackie unfolds her ordinary looking frame and lifts herself from the couch. She looks out the window at her understated landscaping and humble garden. The swaying wind chimes reflect the sun and she hears them sing a delicate song. She takes in another long breath, holds it for a moment and looks at Elsie letting it out.

Elsie holds her breath knowing Jackie has much more to say. She crosses her legs and rests her head on her fist, "I'm ready for my speech."

"You know me Elsie, I don't believe in God the way you do. I know there is one but I believe we all have our own convictions." She sits on the couch and grabs Elsie's hands, "Honey, listen to yourself." Jackie tilts her head, "Even if I used your own Bible against that statement I don't know you'd understand."

Elsie's eyes water and she lets out air saying, "But the Bible *does* say God hates divorce."

"Elsie you know grandpa was a preacher and he made us all go to church and listen to him. I remember the one that said something like, "Don't provoke your kids to anger or for anger; I don't know, something like that."

She points up with two fingers, "And two, as for Esau, how's the one where He's to love you like Christ loved the church." Now would Christ be goin' around beaten the tar outta everyone?"

Elsie lets out a muffled laugh.

"Geez Elsie, I mean Jesus turned the water into wine but he didn't go drinkin' it all up and explode like a nuclear bomb when one of the disciples didn't do what he said."

"But I love him, Jackie. Esau is all I know. I got seven mouths to feed and that's enough to make me so tired, I ain't got time to get a job. And if I did, who would take care of my kids?

"Elsie, darlin' y'all can come live with us."

Elsie stands up and runs her hand in a figure eight around the hanging wall carpet. She feels the tingling sensation of the soft thread. "I love your place, it looks like something outta a magazine or a TV show — she pauses not wanting to admit what she's thinking. "Jackie I love you-ins but I can't see myself with anyone else but Esau — or worse yet — alone." Elsie picks up a framed photo of her and Jackie dressed identical. They were close in age and often mistaken as twins when they were children.

"Sometimes I think I know what you're feeling, Elsie, that's why I went to get you."

"Thank you for rescuin' me, Jackie, at least for a little while."

"I'm sorry you had to go through that abuse when you were fourteen with that horrible guy that took advantage and..."

"...you don't have to finish, I know you were there for me and always will be. Esau always throws that in my face. Shoulda never told him I lost my...my..."

"It's okay, Elsie you don't have to finish either. I know you think you don't deserve better. If Esau tells *you'll never find a better man* to you enough times you'll believe it. ...and really you don't need another man. You can make it on your own, you have family...you have me."

As much as Elsie tried she couldn't conceal the havoc that was raging in her life. Elsie gives in and with a mind-reading look she shoots at Jackie she plops back down.

Jackie stands up to turn off the television that was turned down with a game show playing. "I'd rather see you alone than you or one of the kids dead, Elsie. You'll get over him." She sits closer to Elsie. "You're still young and beautiful. Whenever you walk into a room, men can't take their eyes off you." Jackie looks as if she has a revelation, "Guess that's probably why he's so jealous and keeps you isolated."

"Who's gonna want an instant family of seven, Jackie?" Elsie looks puzzled, tired and hopeless. The dark circles around her eyes are sunken in. "Let's say you're right, soon as he'd find out I left, he'd chase me down and romance me back."

Jackie laughs, "Honey there ain't one stinkin' romantic bone in that man's evil good for nothin' body. She puts her hand on her hip, "He so fulla himself he thinks the sun comes up justa watch him crow."

"What he'd do is hunt you down like a dog and shoot you." She pretends to hold a rifle aiming at Elsie. *"Pow."* She opens her eye back up from squinting and continues looking at her with a tilted head.

Elsie holds her hand up as if to stop the fake bullet with a cynical look.

A siren wails down the street coming from an ambulance that isn't visible, "I don't wanna ever have to see you in one of those."

Elsie looks at Jackie with a somber stare.

To make her point she says, "On your first date when he confessed he killed a cat outta anger it shoulda told you something."

Elsie wipes her face with her hands in anticipation, "Here it comes, oh boy."

Jackie stands up, makes a fist, bends her arm, pulls it back and forward quick, "Golly gee, he told me he killed a cat outta anger, that's swell. He's gonna make an excellent husband who will be kind to my children." She raises one eyebrow, "I'll take this one home, yeah buddy he's a real prize." She pretends to hold up a prize winning fish with a throw pillow. "Real catch this one."

Elsie raises her eyebrows, smiles big, takes the pillow and whacks Jackie over the head with it.

"You're not always funny and you can't make me laugh."

Jackie reaches around and grabs another throw pillow, "Oh, so you want World War III huh?" Jackie pulls the pillow back and Elsie dodges the blow.

"Missed." Elsie is cackling, "Gosh I can't remember the last time I laughed like this." She leans back and claps her hands together once with delight.

Jackie ties to wallop Elsie on the other side and Elsie dodges again, "Can't believe I missed again. Not funny? Well you're sure laughing awful hard," Jackie puts her hand on her chest to catch her breath from laughing too.

Instantly Elsie feels a dread in the pit of her stomach knowing she'll have to return home to the chaos of what is her marriage and raising her children.

Jackie notices the switch and tries cheering her up, "I ain't afraid of that Esau sis. Got half-a sense to hunt him like a rabbit and leave you holdin' one foot for good luck."

"Oh Jackie, you will do no such thing." She chuckles, turns her face and stares at the floor in a daze. Terror once again washes over her and the most horrific vision of having to return from this oasis flashes before her. *"I have no other choice."*

"Are you okay, Elsie?"

"I gotta go home, Jackie." Elsie gets up from the couch and starts gathering her belongings.

"Please stay another day. You need your rest. You don't have to leave so soon. I have plans for us for the rest of the day. I wanna go to the new boutique in town…get you something to wear real nice and practical..." Jackie motions with her hands, "Not over the top, my treat. I wanna have lunch at the new café too, it's owned by a Frenchman that has incredible baked goods. He's famous for his buttery croissants and... Elsie?" Jackie looks concerned.

Eerily Elsie doesn't say another word. With robotic motions she continues putting her belongings in a bag with an instant turn of emotionless movement. "Bring me the baby I gotta go."

"All you had was coffee. You haven't eaten. Let me make you some breakfast before I take you home...or we can eat out."

Elsie turns her back on Jackie to pack up her things she had nearby, "Don't wanna eat. Take me back home. I gotta go home."

"Elsie what just happened here, you were laughing one minute and now..."

She stares at Jackie and in a chilling tone says, "Mind your business, Jackie. Take care of your own."

# Chapter 8

## *The only way out*

"Mommy-ee." Sadie, George, Joseph and Butch all run to Elsie as she walks in the front door of the chicken coop. She slams the door shut and the hook rattles against the door jam.

She hears water dripping from the sink *drip, drip.* The odor of the baby's soiled diaper rose up to her as she took a breath and she turned her head. *"Already?"*

"Mommy, mommy, mommy," Their arms are extended ready to hug their mother as they laugh and shout with happiness. Evan and Ann start to get up but look at Elsie's face and sit back down on the chair watching as the others grab onto Elsie's legs, arms and waist.

"Where's your father?" Elsie looks around the room with apprehension turning her head side to side leaning each time.

"He hasn't been home for a long time today, mommy. Evan points to himself and to each one,

"Me, George, Ann and Sadie been takin' care of the little ones."

Elsie has a glazed look in her eyes only Evan and Ann seem to notice. She throws the baby's belongings on the floor and tells Sadie to hold John. "Here, hold him, gotta git somethin'."

George walks backwards and in front of Elsie trying to talk to her. "So me, Evan and Ann all went to the crick and played on a tree and then, and then, we, uh, we…"

"Get outta my *way* George." Elsie's peculiar behavior is like the volcano's pressure beneath the earth's crust waiting to cause a meltdown. Like the magma is constant in trying to force itself to the surface, so is Elsie's rage.

Sadie stands there holding John with her mouth open unsure of what was happening. The baby has been crying from the moment Elsie walks in.

Evan looks at Ann puzzled and worried, *"Mommy's actin' funny."*

Joseph and Butch sit on the floor in silence, out of Elsie's way.

"You never let me tell you anything." George stomps off angry and plunks himself down on the chair crossing his arms, "I hate you." He kicks Joseph who is almost three and makes him cry.

"What'd you do that for, George? You're always so mean," Evan shouts. He coughs and calms himself to make sure Elsie doesn't go after him now for yelling.

Sadie bounces John up and down in a gentle motion, "sh, sh, sh." She whispers, "Sh, John." Sadie tries to console him by putting her pinky in his mouth.

John screams louder now that Elsie isn't holding him anymore. "Waah," his fists are shaking and his legs are flailing from the discomfort of a dirty diaper and an empty belly.

Elsie pulls the kitchen drawer open. It makes a screeching sound and she reaches in to pull out a large sharp butcher knife. "You-ins ain't worth the powder and lead it takes to blow your brains out." The blade caught some light and flashed in her eyes as she stared at it with a blank look.

The room falls into a complete silence and only John is crying. Sadie sucks in a quick breath in a high pitch squeal escapes her throat at the same time. With nervous hands she reaches for John's pacifier as it keeps rolling away from her until she picks it up, wipes it on her shirt and shoves it in the baby's mouth. John suckles loud, moaning, and is oblivious to his surroundings.

Elsie has resolve in her eyes almost as if she were possessed by something, "Get over here every one of you-ins." Her hair has coiled strands all around her face and some on the top of her head. Her countenance is gaunt with exhaustion. Dark circles surround her eyes making the light green pop out even more. *"This is the only way out."* She grabs hold of Evan's shoulders and forces him into a spot to her left. "Now, y'all are gonna line up as I say."

Evan begins to sob jerking from fear trying to gain control but he can't. It causes a chain reaction with the

65

rest of the children. They figure if their fearless older brother is crying they are in danger.

With the knife in one hand she takes her free hand and lines George up shoulder to shoulder to Evan. *"I can't take this anymore. He ain't gonna hurt them anymore, he ain't gonna hurt me."*

George angles his head back and looks up at his mother towering over him as he's trembling. His big green eyes are spouting out tears, looking into hers, speaking to her — telling her he's remorseful for ever having said he hated her. The tears are almost projectile; like small fountains spewing salty drops down onto his green flannel hand me downs.

"C'mere, Sadie." Sadie tries setting the baby down. "No, bring the baby too."

The children are horrified and sob louder still, breathing in shallow short breaths with their cries. They're covered with tears, trying to resist moving to wipe mucus from their faces.

*"Oh, mommy no not the baby, please mommy."* Sadie takes the baby from a horizontal position to a vertical position and touches John cheek to cheek letting the baby's head rest on her shoulder. John begins to get fussy again, sensing Sadie's fear and hearing the cries. *"Sh, sh, sh, try to be quiet, baby."* Sadie is patting his back trying to calm herself too. The baby spits out the pacifier and lets out a loud hair-raising scream. His tongue is rippling and his fists are shaking in immense distress.

Elsie's breasts begin to lactate, causing soreness making her more annoyed. She hears the blood rushing in her ears, the boisterous hum is deafening in her head, "I wish everyone of you-in's would all die and go straight to hell."

Ann knows she is next and is standing with her hands clinched tight in an awkward stiff posture.

"Ann, stand next to Sadie." Ann hesitates. "Hurry up you little rip." She pushes Ann's shoulder to Sadie's.

*"Mommy, why are you doing this? Daddy is the bad one, why are you doing this to us?"* Ann is angry in part but a lot more anguished, *"God, please help me. Mom is tired and she isn't thinking straight. I need your help. Please God."*

She stood Joseph up from sitting and lined him next to Ann. Joseph's light green eyes mirror Elsie's. He's not sure what is going on but knows he's in a heap of trouble. His mouth is wide open with drool on both sides, hanging midair. He's motioning to his mother he wants to be held. He's curling his little fingers grabbing as if to say, *"C'mere, hold me."* He doesn't understand why she doesn't want to comfort him. Elsie keeps pushing him back in line until Ann grabs his little hand to hold him still.

John continues to cry, gargling on his own saliva. Sadie is trying to quiet him but isn't successful. *"You're makin' her madder, please hush."*

*"Hurry."* Elsie hurries to pick up Butch, swings him around with his small legs in the air and sets him right next to Joseph. Like Joseph, Butch is unaware as to why his mother is being indifferent and cold. Joseph hugs Butch and Butch hangs onto him too. Elsie is unmoved by this picture. *"You won't have to suffer anymore."*

Evan, Sadie and Ann, take turns begging Elsie not to hurt them. "Mommy, you're scaring us. What are you doing? Please."

She points to Butch and tells Sadie, "Set the baby right next to Butch." She looks at the butcher knife, "I'm gonna kill every one of you-ins, then kill the baby, and then kill myself."

They all scream louder bobbing up and down in an anxious horror as if they had to go to the bathroom. They couldn't resist moving.

George screams, "No."

The baby is worked up from crying and vomits on Sadie. *"Oh no, John."*

She grabs George, "I'm gonna kill you first cuz you're the meanest." She put the knife to George's throat.

He puts his hands up to protect himself, "Oh, please mommy, no." George feels a trickle down his leg as a stream of urine escapes him from absolute terror. He doesn't dare look down at his pants for fear of incurring greater harm.

Elsie in a frenzied state overlooks their stress and continues to line them.

"No," George screams again, "No, mommy, please don't kill me." George is trying hard not to move. The trail of urine on the inside of his pants spread more. He felt the heated steady stream on his legs and squirmed subtly. The children are restless and in the biggest fright of their short lives.

"Everyone shut up and be still." She shrieks with a loud voice wanting to get this over with. "We're wastin' time."

The cries were horrifying almost as though a slaughter house of animals were being massacred.

She raises the knife looking at George's neck.

A streak of lightning ripples through the sky. A thunderous clap roars, *crash* and Elsie jumps.

George jumps when she does, "Ah, no," he yells.

She feels a gentle breeze come in through the cracks of the door. A presence is encompassing her. Warmth touches her as she feels an intense burden is lifted off. She can almost hear a whisper, *"Elsie."* It envelops her as she pauses in midair to take in its splendor. She is not sure if she is hallucinating from a lack of sleep but this presence she senses brings her back to sanity.

Frozen from shock, Elsie drops the knife and falls to her knees sobbing, quaking hysterically. Her face is buried in her hands. She only cries and doesn't say a word. She rocks on her knees back and forth covering her face in shame.

Ann is not sure what was surrounding her mother but whatever it was she was sure it stopped Elsie from slaying her family. Ann senses an ambiance of a supernatural being, *"Is this you God? Did you hear my prayer?"*

The children are terrified to make one move. They aren't sure if she'd pick the knife back up again and lunge forward on them. They stand with stifled whimpers broken and slouched.

She looks up at the children. "You-ins make me so mad."

They all look at each other puzzled.

She reaches out to pick up John. She rocks him and cries, "Sh, sh, sh."

"Mama, you look real tired. Maybe you need a nap," Evan says yet still bewildered from the trauma.

George didn't forget the knife to his throat. He asks permission with reverence. "Yeah, mommy can we play outside before daddy gets home?"

With an immense sorrow and a haunting remorse she never verbalizes. She says, "Soon as you see your daddy comin' around run back in."

# Chapter 9

# *Child's Play*

T hey run towards the door to take a shot at who gets to go outside first. Sadie takes advantage of the baby's exhaustion and puts him to sleep in the basket. Elsie's eyes are burning and heavy with fatigue, "Go play outside and you can change when you come back in." In an instant Elsie pours herself into the bed next to the baby and begins to take in deep breaths almost snoring—she is forcing out air through her mouth. "Puh." Elsie has surrendered to a profound slumber.

Evan screams, "Hey let's take our shoes off."

Ann hushes Evan with her finger to her lips, "Shush."

The children all freeze as if they were playing a game. This time they were trying not to awaken their tired and volatile mother.

Elsie isn't moved.

They fall to the ground in a hurry to take their shoes and socks off.

Ann was the first one out the door. "Ray..." Her arms are waving over her head like a chimpanzee before she takes a spill from the slippery wet grass. Giggling on the ground she continues, "Rain." Ann whips back up and spots a tree. "Watch me climb that tree."

When Ann wanted to leave the chicken coop or something *bad* would happen to her she would day-dream of climbing the tallest tree she could find. She would envision she was on top of the world where no harm was lurking. She often shared her dreams with Sadie and they would both laugh at the silliness but comforted by their stories. Any time Ann had an opportunity to slip out or allowed to play outdoors, she would find the nearest tree and carry out her goal. It was an exhilarating moment. She felt unstoppable when she reached the top branches.

Ann spots the best tree to climb near the house and sees all the potential limbs needing to be climbed in order to reach the top, "You're the one." It was more than tree climbing to her but a getaway. She had her eye on a red mulberry tree. It was about 60 feet in height and 2 feet in diameter. It had a short dense trunk but a spreading crown. She was lured by a fleshy cluster of mulberries resembling blackberries. Some were immature and red instead of being darker but she continued gathering. She knew the best tasting ones turned deep purple when ripe in mid-summer; sweet, juicy and edible. The sides of her mouth stung from watering.

Still inside, Butch's blue eyes are so tired they almost cross as he leans over on the floor in slow motion next to the baby and falls asleep too.

George follows behind Ann. He screams as if he discovered grass for the first time, "Grass." He prolongs the letter *a* in grass for a long time and says it again yelling, "Grass." He extends his arms from his sides with palms cupped and lets his face soak in the rain, "The rain is kinda cold, yeah. Feels good."

The door is still open and Joseph is standing there squealing with delight watching the children play. His arms are flapping like a baby bird learning to fly. "Eee, go, go, me go," His knees are bending and popping back up with *go*.

Sadie picks up Joseph on the way out and dangles him over grass until she sets him down.

Joseph jumps up, extends both his small arms like he was a rocketed torpedo into the rain. "Me play, me play. In a high pitched shrill he yells, "Play-ee."

Evan takes a running leap and slides on the grass sideways as if he scored a home run. He's on the ground elated with content.

George follows the same trail and tries sliding like Evan bumping into him in the end, "I caught up to you, ha." They begin to wrestle in the rain with laughter.

"Look up here y'all." Ann is sitting on the highest branch of the red mulberry tree bouncing up and down waving. "Yeehaw." She opens her mouth and lets her tongue out to taste the rain. Her fingers are purple from picking mulberries and her tongue is turning a lighter violet from the rain washing out the darkest color. Her eyes are blinking taking in the rain too. Her dirty blonde hair forms chunks like a wet mop dripping with water. "I'm on top of the world," She yells as she shakes her head and her dripping hair form small clusters of water around her head.

Sadie decides to slide after Evan and George and she takes a running start but slips and falls. "It's really slippery," she laughs. Her little dress is stuck to her body and is transparent in an adorable way. Her bright blue eyes glisten in the water as she blinks to be able to site her target again. She gets back up and slides into Evan and George to create a huddle and they shake with laughter.

Joseph is running in circles squealing. He's patting both sides of his head at the same time in cadence to his own hasty march, "Eeee, play, eee, play, eee, eee, play." Joseph's diaper is sopping wet with water and sagging in the back. He slips and falls and the diaper makes a gushing blast oozing water from the sides. He chuckles with satisfaction, "ahh, hee." Joseph wipes and clears his light green eyes to focus on the other children and is thrilled by what he sees. He points up to the tree, "Ann, Ann, ooh, ooh."

Ann is hanging from the tree with both hands, "Watch me fly." The tree is dark brown tinged with red and scales of long irregular ridges. She raises and lowers her legs to get a swing going. As soon as she propels herself forward she lets go of the branch and lands on the ground with her knees bent as if she were a gymnast and falls on her rear. She leans back hard on her arms.

Joseph claps excitedly, "eee, eee, eee," he is shrieking with earsplitting sounds of amusement.

He jumps up and stomps into a puddle, "yuh, yuh, yah, yah, ah, ah." The water stings the bottom of his feet. He looks at Ann as he stomps, "Me, me, me."

Ann claps eagerly, "Yeah Joseph."

A slow rumble in the sky lets out an unexpected thunder. The ground trembles from the loudness. Ann yells, "Yeah thunder." She raises her hands as though she were a champion.

Joseph copies yet with mystery, wide eyed and scared, "Thundoo, yeah." His tiny eyes shift back and forth waiting for the next crash.

Ann notices and runs towards him. She pulls out some berries from her pocket and some of the red immature berries are mixed with the ripened ones. They still give off a bitter taste.

Joseph opens his mouth and spits them back out, "bluh...ack." He disapproves with his head, "No more." Ann laughs and takes hold of his little hands and skips in circles. "Ring around the Rosie, pocket full of posies, ashes, ashes, we all fall down."

"Down." Joseph grunts as he falls with Ann. "Again, again, again."

This time Evan, Sadie and George run into the game to be part of the next round. They all chant, "Ring around the Rosie, pocket full of posies, ashes, ashes, we all fall..."

"Down," They yell and drop to the ground, Evan says, "What does that mean anyway."

George shrugs, "I dunno, beats me." He points to the thick tree, "That tree, safe place," He proclaims. He runs towards the large Virginia pine.

"No fair," Ann runs to the tree and beats George to touch it. "Grandma Novak told me it's a nursery rhyme and it's not about the plague like everyone thinks. It was written long after the plague."

George laughs, "Is that what you do when Granma takes you to the library? I thought you sat and looked at the pictures."

Ann chuckles, "No, that's you." They are running side by side and Ann picks up speed.

Evan runs behind George and Sadie gets up to run too.

Joseph is left on the ground and begins to cry from abandonment. Sadie runs back, "Oh baby you wanna play?"

He extends his arms to be carried and rubs his eyes from tiredness, "I think you need a nap." Sadie scoops him up into her adolescent arms.

She takes Joseph back inside, changes his clothes and puts him next to Elsie who is breathing so slow she almost looks dead. Sadie is worried and nudges her with a gentle push. Elsie grunts, turns to her side and continues snoring.

Sadie turns around to go back outside and hears the children's screams are faint and farther way. She opens the door and is shocked.

"Where you goin'? Where's er-body at?" Instead of going inside Esau pulls Sadie outside and pulls her to the car. "No, daddy not again, I don't wanna go, please let me back inside with mommy."

# Chapter 10

# *Tree house*

The rain has slowed and Esau inches the vehicle out into a wooded area slowly. He puts it in park, turns off the ignition and turns to Sadie in the front seat, "I love you Sadie, I'm glad we can be alone again."

"Please no, daddy. Not again, I don't want this." She feels her pulse pounding in her temples and in an instant her palms are cold and sweaty.

The vivid green leaves are dripping with spring rain in the background as Sadie looks past her father. Raindrops are bouncing on the branches and a few wild animals bustle to find shelter. Beads of rain are creating a trace of water pouring down the sides of the windows. Gushing winds make the tall bushes wave and Sadie is suspended for a time. She makes sure to harden her heart towards his advances and not look him in the eye. She hears herself breathing and tries not to create hysteria or anything else to worsen the consequences.

"Your eyes are blue Sadie, you're not mine. You can be my girlfriend."

"I'm too young to be anyone's girlfriend. Besides my eyes are the same as grandmas. And I *hate* you when you do that to me." She folds her arms and covers as much of her body as she can so he'll stop looking at her.

"But you shake at the end like you like it, Sadie. Don't you?"

"No I don't like you touching me." She twists her whole body to pull his arm away.

"This time you can rub me anyway you want, Sadie."

She starts trembling with anger and crying gritting her teeth, "You're doing this to Ann too aren't you?"

"Ann doesn't love me like you do. She screams cries and kicks and never lets me do anything to her. She won't love me back."

"It's cuz she doesn't love you. I don't either. You promised me if I let you do this you wouldn't hurt any of the others."

"Ann won't let me so I haven't."

"You're not listening; I don't want you to try either. Leave her alone." She yells, "Don't mess with her."

She punches his chest.

Esau grabs her face and starts to kiss her. Sadie moans with dread and continues crying. He reaches under her dress between her legs.

Her body begins to betray her.

"See, I know you love me Sadie."

She closes her eyes tight and daydreams, *I'm not here; I'm in a tree house playing. There are sticks tied up with knots dangling from my house. I'm climbing with Ann and we're looking at the different color boards I painted. We'll use the stairs later. I built them to wrap around like a coil until reaching the top of the tree.* "*C'mon, Ann, bring your dolls I'll make them cardboard houses.*"

"*Okay, Sadie, you're my hero, you always rescue me.*"

Tears stream down Sadie's face as Esau pleasures himself while touching her.

"*I know, Ann, we'll be safe here. Daddy can't touch us up here. We have guards on the ground and we are the only ones with the key to get in. The key to this playhouse heaven is imagination.*"

"*Sadie, I can't believe how huge this tree is and how green the leaves are. Where did you find this place? Do the others know about it? It's so wonderful. There are thousands of trees like it everywhere.*"

"*No one knows, Ann, this is our heaven. I built it for us. It's perfect weather all year around. It's not hot or cold, the breeze from the windows feel amazing. There is a crystal river nearby that glistens in the sun and it's always warm, you can see it through this window.*"

"*I love the lace curtains, and the little stove and sink, and all the little ceramic dishes to have tea parties. Oh, and look at the little sofa with soft green stuff on it. I especially love this table with the chairs and our own color TV. It's gotta indoor bathroom.*

*"Why don't you pick up your lace gloves and put them on, Ann; they go up to your elbow. We can get ready for our tea party."*

*"Oh, alright, but you know I'm a tomboy. I'll do it just or you."*

*"I'll get our hats and scarves, Sadie. I love what you built."*

*"I have some fancy dolls, Ann, like the ones Aunt Jackie collects that she doesn't let us play with. We can seat them next to your rag dolls."*

*"I'll think they'll all get along fine, Sadie. I love you."*

"I love you Sadie. Tell me you love me." Esau notices Sadie is distant and wants her to stay in the moment. She refuses and keeps her eyes closed and head turned away.

"I love you, *Ann.*"

*"Grab the large hats and feather scarves. This is a special honey and vanilla tea with butter crackers. Pinkies up, grab your cup...let the tea party begin. Shall we, Ann?"*

*"Shall we? hee hee, you're a silly sister, Sadie."*

*"Oh look, your rag dolls are coming to life. The fancy dolls are too."*

*"No they're not, Sadie."*

*"Yes, Ann, use your imagination and escape with me."*

*"I'll get the cookies from the cabinet. Where did you get these cookies Sadie?"*

*"That's great, Ann. Take a look inside. I have any-thing you want in these cupboards. They're magic. Look out the window at the red bikes we'll ride Ann.*

*We'll take the trail and bring the magic picnic basket. We'll pick up the stray kittens we've always wanted. I remember the colorful one."*

*"I remember it too; mom didn't let us keep it."*

*"We'll keep the kittens here in our house Ann. We'll all be safe and we'll never be hungry."*

*"I'll open the basket Sadie, what's inside?"*

*"Oh, it has candy and all the food you want like hotdogs, cheeseburgers, French fries, and pizza."*

*"French fries, Sadie? Pizza? Tee hee, you're funny."*

*"Let's take the spiral stairs this time and ride our bikes, Ann."*

*"I can't ride a bike, Sadie."*

*"Funny girl, you mean you can see the imaginary red bike but you can't ride it?"*

*"I forget I have the key. Guess I could fly if I wanted too huh, Sadie."*

*"We can have a picnic when we land, Ann."*

*"Now that's the silliest idea of them all, Sadie."*

*"We'll eat and do anything we want. You think that's silly? We'll make ice cream cones with sprinkles and we'll…"*

This time Esau tries to lie on top of Sadie while still pleasing himself.

*"Ann, help me. Help me."*

Sadie sees herself falling from the tree. She's brought back to this instant to fight for her purity and for her life. She pushes him away with repugnance but he continues with his hand.

Esau is moaning and sweaty and finishes before he can accomplish his goal to mar her purity. He's breathing heavily, "Don't tell your mother or she'll kill me then you kids will be taken away and have no one."

Sadie pulls his hand away in disdain. His hair cream smells good yet she's repulsed by the fact she likes the smell.

"You didn't shake, let me make you shake."

"No. I don't wanna, I wanna go home," Sadie exclaims.

Esau insists and puts his hand back under her dress with a menacing tone, "I'll kill you if you don't let me."

A faint sound of children laughing is in the distance.

"Sadie." Ann is yelling Sadie's name, "Sadie."

Sadie hears *Ann's* voice in a distance. *"Oh thank God, you heard my thoughts."*

# Chapter 11

# *Hikey*

Ann and Sadie are walking on the crunchy autumn leaves beneath their feet. Rumored snow is about to fall in the next few days. Their chore was appalling; nonetheless, it needed to be done before the looming storm crept in.

"I hate it when we gotta rinse out these diapers, Sadie, yuck," Ann yells.

The meandering trails were picturesque like a geographic magazine. What people envy to vacation to, was the background Ann and her family grew up in.

"And two buckets fulla 'em too, Ann." Sadie glances up and around at the canopy of vines they are passing.

The creek water was low and clear in the hollow between the Virginia mountains. Fall beech, sugar maple and diverse oak trees are slanted on the slopes and outline the trails of the narrow dirt roads. Their shadows followed them and the multicolored leaves spun around as if they were twirling ballerinas falling from the trees in random sequence. Ann kicked an acorn a few feet in front of her, when she caught up to it she kicked it again. She got bored with it then kept busy by kicking a bottle cap until she put it in her pocket.

"Can't believe we gotta walk all this way in these hollers to rinse off hikey." Ann is sulking with each step.

"Mom was afraid to walk all the way out here with the log bridge bein' washed out an all." Sadie is trying to justify the reason they walked, for what seemed like miles, to rinse diapers. "What if she got stuck with all us out here?" She shrugs and holds out her hands as if to solve a mystery.

Ann looks at her with a puzzled look with one sarcastic eyebrow raised, "She should rinse 'em outside the house, Sadie then put 'em in the washer with the rest of the clothes."

Ann has her hand on her hip, "We're lucky dad don't make us clean the outhouse, he does that himself. And know what else, Sadie?"

Sadie motions *no*.

"Ever notice wherever we move he always finds homes with outhouses. Hows come we never get to use a toilet?"

Sadie shrugs.

The trail was winding down in large circles until they reached the side of the mountain where the creek was located. At the time one other family lived within a few miles away. Their father made sure to seclude them as much as possible to keep them under his thumb. It didn't matter if they had neighbors, they were still isolated. As soon as his obsession with moving set in, for sheer manipulation he would move them. Not a soul could tell what was happening. The entire family could've been obliterated and no one would have ever known the Flinks. Esau was good at getting himself thrown out of places and banned for life. He always encountered people gullible enough to believe his sincerity—but when they saw what was beneath, they fled as far as the east is from the west away from him. For Esau there was no pardon. One gains true forgiveness when there is sincere repentance, there never was.

"Yeah Ann but there's so much hikey in here. It'll stink up the backyard. At least we get to go out and get away from dad."

Ann widens her eyes, "Yeah, that alone is worth the *hikey.*"

Sadie throws her head back and laughs shaking her finger, "Don't let dad catch you swearin' like that or you'll be drinkin' turpentine."

She waves at Sadie with a dismissive gesture. "Oh, I know silly, I might as well say the "s" word as bad as he thinks it is to say hikey."

Sadie squints her eyes.

"Just kidding with you, you know I don't cuss. Forget about him. Don't wanna *think* about him." Ann jerks her head side to side and shivers in revulsion, "uck."

Ann has a pensive look, "Sadie, besides dad always yelling and hitting all of us, is there any other reason why you don't wanna be around him?"

Sadie coughs, "I'd rather talk about hikey."

Ann interprets her comment to mean either Sadie knows nothing about Esau's inappropriate ways or she doesn't want to say, *"She probably doesn't know, I better not tell her anything. Then she'll tell mom and I'll get into big trouble."*

"Oh look, Ann, here are some nice sticks we can use to pick up the diapers so we don't have to touch the hikey."

They both giggle and look at each other, "I bet we say *hikey* more these days than we will our whole lives. Huh, Sadie?"

Ann jumps near the creek with her bucket. "Okay, then we won't call it hikey."

She dumps the diapers at the edge of the creek and Sadie is watching. "What are you doin Ann."

"Ever notice how mushy it is?"

Sadie scrunches her nose with a gag reflex. "I'm gonna puke." She doubles over, "thwuah."

Ann laughs, "Just pretend you're 'bout to take some bad medicine so you don't gotta smell it."

"Unkay that's better." Sadie turns her bucket upside down and each of them comes plopping out forming a mound of messy cloth diapers. Some of the feces splash onto one of her shoes. "Oh God help me, ung-thwuah."

Ann says with an amusing laugh, "Oh crap. Eeww rinse it off in the crick and try not to smell it."

Ann gets on her knees and takes a handful of feces that is still a bit hardened. She squeezes with her entire hand letting it ooze from between her fingers. "Look, tooth paste."

"Ung-thwuah." Sadie's nostrils flare, her tongue ripples with a gag reflex and she turns her head to put her arm over her nose. Her eyes water, "Ann, that's just sick."

Ann laughs like a high pitched opera singer singing the same ringing note.

"You try it. It's like that colored clay stuff we got from the poke once, before it dried up."

Sadie is revolted, "It's not clay though it's, it's..."

"Hikey." Ann laughed until she couldn't bare it anymore. She takes more feces and squeezes it out of both hands. "You know how people say don't eat the yellow snow, we should tell people, don't drink from the hollers crick."

Sadie reaches down with a beleaguered look and pinches some out of one hand trying to hold her breath. "You better not ever tell anyone we did this, thwuah."

"I'd cross my heart but I got my hands in some..." She stops to lift her hand and looks at it front and back. "Hikey," Ann giggles and teases Sadie, "C'mon Sadie it's just baby poop. We get it all over our hands when we scrub the diapers anyway."

"We better get back before mom starts wonderin' what's goin' on. Plus you're cussing too much Ann."

"What? Hikey, hikey, hikey, you likey the hikey." Ann is laughing at her joke until her face turns red.

Ann and Sadie got back in time to see snowflakes start to fall. "Burr, no wonder it got cold all of the sudden, it's starting to come down already." Ann is looking out of the window.

Evan says, "It's the sticky kinda snow too. Mom you think we can all go play in it later before dad gets home. He's workin' real late again anyway ain't he?"

"Soon as you-ins get your chores done you can go play in the snow — 'sides it's Saturday, don't see why not."

Evan and George start picking up clothes and shoes scattered around. Sadie and Ann offer to do the dishes since they had a finger nail growing contest. They knew if they had their hands in soapy water it made their nails grow faster.

Sadie smiles at Ann, "If you lose you'll hafta scratch my back for a *whole* week."

Ann returns the smile and nods, "Deal. And if you lose you hafta wash the dishes for a *whole* week."

They prepare the sink with dish soap and warm water. As the bubbles begin to form Sadie starts to sing. She closes her eyes and a rich tone reverberates in her head and chest while she sings her line with refinement. *"I've got my eye on you, so please don't make me blue, and if you feel it too just say, I love you."*

*"And if you make me cry, I'll have to say goodbye, I need a reason why, to say I love you."* Ann's voice cracked with a slight yodel and was sharp as she shrieked all the way through her line. She gets irritated with herself, "You have the better singing voice. I'll leave that to you."

"Oh Ann, everybody is good at something. We're doin' it for fun anyway."

The snow was falling with fat flakes swirling in different directions. Inches of snow accumulating on the ground made the children rush to finish and play outside before Esau got home. They could hear the wheezing air filtering through the cracks of the window and door crevices. The flakes of snow slapped against the windows sticking to the corners looking like a picturesque Christmas card. The ground can no longer be seen through layers of glittery white snow. It shimmered with traces of blue when the sun reflected at an angle.

Evan announces, "I'm done, can we go now."

Elsie smiles, "ee-yep."

Evan, George, Sadie, Ann and Joseph all run to their coats, boots and socks turned into makeshift gloves.

George says, "I saved some cardboard boxes we can use to slide down the snowy mountain."

The children are excited they get to play in the first heavy snow of the year.

They all file outside ready to slide down the snow laden mountain. They feel blessed to have clothes, boots and extra socks to keep their hands and feet warm since Esau had a better job and worked longer hours.

They were all bundled up from head to toe barely able to see their eyes. George being the heaviest waddled when he walked.

Almost at the top of the hill Evan laughs at George, "You look like the Michelin man."

"Shut up stupid." George ignores Evan and points, "Look, a hood of an old car," He shrieks.

"Redneck sleddin. Yeehaw," Sadie yells and laughs.

Evan and George grab each end of the car hood and throw it to the ground on the snowy mountainside. Fresh tire marks of a few vehicles lead the sledding route. Not realizing how dangerous their stunts are they set the hood on the narrow icy road.

"Guess you gotta sit down in it." Ann gets in first with excitement.

"I found it I wanna ride first, you push Evan." George jumps in.

"Oh alright I'll push the first time."

Sadie and Joseph both climb into the large hood. Evan pushes them down the slope with a grunt. "There you go suckers."

The four children aren't expecting the hood to speed down the incline at such a high velocity and all begin screaming with exhilaration. They hear the hood scraping in the snow.

George yells, "Yippee," He has a look of horror, "Oh no we're headed for that huge white oak. Ah, no." His breathing races.

Right before the car hood hits the tree on the side of the road it whips around and goes back on the trail. After holding their breaths they all sigh with relief.

"Wow, this is goin' *fast*." The hood begins to spin and gains momentum. "Oh no, look, a rock," Ann shouts.

The weighty metal sled approaches the rock and rams into it sending them skyward for a few seconds. They scream as the hood lands with a great thud.

They hear a screeching cry. "Shoot, we lost Joseph." Sadie tries to look back at Joseph but the sled is moving and spinning too fast. "We'll be back for you Joseph." Sadie is watching the swirling view.

Evan falls to his knees with laughter at the hilarity of a speeding hood soaring and watching Joseph flying off. He's pounding on the road, "Gosh this is better than a movie, wish we could afford a camera."

He trails off into a thought. *"I wanna do something with my life. None of us'll finish school I bet—maybe I'll finish. I'll make somethin of myself; I'll never be like him. I hate him. I'm gonna be somebody. I'll buy cameras and all the stuff I need and want.*

Joseph fell on a soft patch to the side and came up out of the snow unharmed. He's coughing like he had been for a few days.

At the bottom of the mountain the girls get up to check on Joseph. The rest are laughing and breathing hard from the rush of the speeding sled. They drag the hood back up the mountain. George remembers he has something in his pocket.

He reaches into his coat and pulls out a homemade gadget, "I got something I wanna try out." He has a huge grin on his face. "Evan, shoot me with this gun."

Ann looks worried, "What for, George? Why you want Evan to hurt you."

Evan smiles, "Be my pleasure sucker."

"I wanna see if it works. Shoot me."

Ann, the voice of reason is concerned, "George, you're takin' this too far, let's stick to playing."

"No, I wanna see if I made it strong enough. Pull that big rubber band back, but do it hard, Evan."

"You are so stupid, George." Evan pulls back the rubber band with the pellet in it and aims at George's leg.

"I'm gonna count to three and shoot."

George stands with his legs apart and body tightened ready for the shot. He has his pant leg rolled up and he's pulling out his skin for Evan to shoot. "Right here Evan, shoot between here."

Evan nods, "You are one twisted person."

"One, two…"

George squints, his eyes closed.

"Pop." George flinches, "You dummy you didn't release the band."

Evan thinks scaring him is comical. "Man, you flinched especially when I yelled *pop*. You sure you wanna do this?"

"C'mon, Evan, do it."

"One, two…"

George lets out a yelp. "Ah." George jumps on one leg, "You didn't say three."

Evan is crowing with laughter at George, pointing to his leg.

George looks down at his leg. There is a bloody hole now where his skin is pierced. He pulls back on the loose skin and smiles, "It works. Hows come if I'm stupid, Evan this gun I made…well it wouldn't hurt me."

Ann condemns with folded arms.

"Evan laughs at George you gotta be the dumbest kid I know."

"Oh shush, Evan, you ain't got friends, what are, you talkin' about."

Ann shakes her head, "Both of you are crazy, it's your turn, Evan let's go."

"Can't wait to see the look on mom and dad's face when you tell them you shot yourself," Evan laughs.

"You shot me dummy," George says.

"You told me to."

# Chapter 12

# *Following signs and wonders*

J oseph was struggling to breathe. He began coughing with a loud bark as if he were a seal. Elsie touched his forehead and said, "He's burning up." She was also concerned at the panicked look in Joseph's eyes as he tried with great effort to breathe. His cheeks were covered with rosy blotches. In trying to stand up he became dizzy and disoriented.

"We better get him to the hospital Esau. He don't look good."

"Evan, take care of the kids while we take Joseph to the hospital. We'll take a couple with us and you can watch the rest. Lock the door." Elsie turned around and followed Esau out to their vehicle to take Joseph to the hospital.

Evan and the rest of the children had fretful looks on their faces and noticed Joseph's lifeless and pale look was worsening. They stole a peak out of the window to watch Esau carry Joseph's almost unresponsive body.

As soon as Joseph was admitted the concerned nurses put Joseph in an oxygen tank at Doctors orders.

"Nurse please start an I.V. immediately, he's dehydrated." The Dr. looks at Elsie, "Ma'am I don't know how long he's been sick but his blood pressure is dangerously low and so are his oxygen levels. These levels are so low he could potentially have brain damage or worse, not make it through the night."

Elsie asks, "Is he going to be alright?"

The Doctor is focused and doesn't respond to Elsie.

The nurse responds looking at the critical symptoms and vital signs, "Do you have a church or minister we can call?"

Elsie shakes her head no.

The canopy of the oxygen tent was made of transparent PVC. It was rigged on a frame, suspended over a hospital bed and tucked underneath the mattress with zipped openings giving access to the child. The tent cooled patients and was also used for oxygen therapy. A compressor-powered refrigeration unit was positioned beside the bed and a cooling cabinet fitted under it. The system was sealed and contained liquid Freon.

The nurse had a genuine concern and stepped out to her desk to make a phone call. She picks up the receiver on the rotary phone and dials a number and proceeds, "Yes, is this Pastor Charles? ...Hi, this is nurse Wiley from the hospital... Uh-huh yes, God bless you too pastor. We have a young boy here named Joseph Flink who has the croup and is in an oxygen tent... Yes, sad I know. He's in critical condition with low levels of blood pressure and oxygen… Um, Dr. Walsh, well, he doesn't expect him to make it through the night. I thought since these people told me they didn't go to church maybe you could come out here to pray… Great, we'll be expecting you."

Elsie is touching the edge of John's bed, "God will send an angel to heal you."

Esau is in the lobby with the rest of the children, he is wracked with worry. *"Lord I know I ain't been perfect, but please help my boy. I'll do whatever it takes for him to feel better."*

He has his head buried in both hands with a sense of fault. He is conflicted by this awareness since he never thinks of anyone else but himself. He's not sure if he should blame Elsie for letting Joseph play outdoors while sick or blame himself. He is in an abyss of narcissism. It's easier for him to obsess about facing another drink than facing his feelings.

Pastor Charles arrives minutes later; He takes his hat off in reverence of being indoors. "Hi my name is Pastor Charles Begley and I'd like to pray with Joseph Flink."

He tucks his hat under his arm without crushing it.

"Yes Pastor I know who you are; I'm the one who phoned you, right this way." Nurse Wiley leads the pastor to Joseph's room."

While walking, Pastor Charles notices how attractive nurse Wiley is but makes sure not to lust after her averting his attention to the pictures on the walls while he walks. Still looking at the walls he says, "Well you look different in your nurses dress and hat than at church, sorry about that."

Nurse Wiley turns and smiles, "It's okay pastor." She continues walking forward. "I get that a lot."

As they enter Joseph's room, the Pastor looks around at the white sterile room and hears the equipment sounds of the oxygen tank at work. Beeping sounds of the different machines are doing their job as they monitor his vital statistics. Joseph is being monitored on all sides. He is unconscious.

Charles turns around and gestures to Elsie with a respectful nod. She is returning from the vending machines with a cup of coffee in her hand, "Ma'am, I'm Pastor Charles Begley and I'm here to pray for lil' Joseph. If you allow me I'd like to lay hands on him."

"You mean pray for him?" She waves in a circle as if to tell him to proceed. "Go ahead; I knew God would send someone." Elsie gives him a curious look. She takes another sip of coffee and sets it on Joseph's brown hospital tray.

Pastor Charles opens his blazer and reaches into his inner pocket to pull out olive oil he always carried with him. He dips his finger and places his balmy hand under the tent on Joseph's belly. He raises his other hand, grooves form on his forehead and with an earnest fervor and authority he exclaims, "Father, we humbly come before you in the name of Jesus."

The atmosphere in the room changes suddenly. Elsie feels goose bumps permeate through her body. She feels warm sensations fill her entire being and almost felt she could see mist all around. She blinks her eyes twice to make sure. Large tears began to spurt out of her eyes. She has the urge to lift her hand too but keeps her arms crossed in reverence.

"We ask that you have mercy over this young man and heal his body. We believe your Word that *heals us by your stripes*. I pray the levels of oxygen and blood pressure will rise instantly in your name. That all organs will function proper the way you designed Lord."

Elsie is wiping her tears with the palms of her hands to make sure to get every drop. *"Wow, what am I feeling?"*

Esau shadows the door of the hospital room. He is curious to see the man who asked about his child. He left the children in the waiting room. Before he can make any judgments he sees the monitors begin to rise, slow and steady. He puts his head down. He is touched in his soul.

"Thank you Jesus, in your name we pray, amen." Pastor Charles turns around; he looks at Esau then at Elsie, "I believe God did a miracle here today. I can feel it. If you fine people don't have a place to worship you can come to my church down the road here.

He motions with his hand and pronounces the one syllable word *left* with two syllables, "It's on your lay-eft. We're the only ones with a tall white steeple and bell tower."

Esau and Elsie both smile wiping their tears. They dry their hands on their clothes.

The next morning Joseph was sitting up in bed, breathing fine on his own and opening a piece of candy Pastor Charles had set on the night stand for him to eat. An envelope was next to the candy. "Mommy, daddy." Joseph hands them the envelope.

*"Mr. & Mrs. Flink, I felt lead of the Lord to leave you this offering for you and your family. Please take this and be blessed."*

Pastor Charles had given them a week's salary from the church. He was always giving his money to either people in need or the sake of the church. He was selfless. He had a giving spirit born out of his genuine love for people. He trusted his faith, knowing God would return it in abundance.

Elsie eyes water as she shows Esau $50 fanned out in tens. "When I saw him put that candy on the stand before he even prayed, I knew he had lotsa faith Joseph would make it through the night." She looked at the nurse's name tag saying, "Nurse Wiley, thank you for calling him."

"No problem Elsie, he's a good man and I go to his church. We see healings like this all the time." Nurse Wiley noticed the envelope and the candy, "That's my pastor."

Nurse Wiley was 50 years of age but her dark complexion made her look as if she was in her thirties. Her skin was smooth and mesmerizing to look at. Her hair was silver. She liked to keep it short in a pixie style. Her eyes were green and attention-grabbing. You couldn't resist staring at her when she talked. She kept her figure and watched her weight because of her diabetes. She made a nurses outfit look like a sexy costume. It was tapered to her well-endowed upper body. Her bottom half had the curves of an acoustic guitar. Whenever she bent over in front of patients she was mindful to put her hand over her chest to not show cleavage.

Nurse Wiley is checking Joseph's vital signs again, "Can you lean forward now so I can listen to your lungs?" She places the stethoscope on Joseph's back, "Good boy, everything is looking and sounding *much* better than last night."

Because Nurse Wiley respected others, and was beautiful and intelligent, it was difficult for people to discriminate against her being a minority. She didn't like being treated as a sex object and had no problems putting men who got out of line in their place. Whenever any of her patients said a comment with a sexual connotation she was ready to quip, *"Thank you sir, this is the body the Lord has made and my husband is the only one who'll be glad in it."*

# Chapter 13

# *No more cancer*

Pastor Charles wasn't rich but because he was a carpenter and liked southern homes, his home appeared luxurious. The picture of southern hospitality Pastor Charles built for his late wife was a rectangular Plantation style home. To accommodate the warm, humid weather of the south, the way he liked it, he made it spacious and airy with high ceilings. It had a large front porch with a series of round columns.

The veranda wrapped all around the house to provide shade throughout the heat of the day. His plans were to welcome visitors with a soaring columned porch where he liked to sit in his wooden chair and had extras for company. He had a wicker table next to his chair with a framed picture and two books on it written by his favorite authors, Charles Spurgeon & Oswald Chambers. He felt as if he were the king of his domain in this home. It had a captivating old world charm.

Although Pastor Charles was Irish he had a southern drawl. He was short and weighed 180 lbs. He had quirky mannerisms yet authoritative from what he called the *anointing* when preaching. Outside of church he was otherwise calm and peaceful—unless he got upset over something. He was quick tempered and he'd say his usual Christian substituted expletive. *"I'm mad as spit, dagnabit."*

Esau and Elsie grew fond of Pastor Charles since the day he prayed for Joseph who received the miracle of life. After a few months of visiting the church and the pastor's home regularly the Flink's started to heal. Their marriage and their children both began to live a normal life which was the true miracle.

It was a morning like any other. As Elsie is getting dressed she notices a seed wart on her knee starting to take a suspicious form. She had Esau drive her to the hospital to have it checked out. The results were devastating. She was told it had turned cancerous. After receiving the news she turned to Esau, "We gotta go to Pastor Charles to pray for my knee. I don't wanna wait for church Sunday."

On the drive home they road home in silence. Esau doesn't know what to say. Elsie is dazed from the news. They walked over to the pastor's house. Esau had moved the family near because of their fondness towards him. Esau is troubled for Elsie, he thinks of holding her hand on their walk. He tries but feels awkward so he lets go. *"What am I gonna do without her? Who's gonna take care of all those kids?"*

Elsie looks at Esau, she wants to grab his arm as they walk but sees Esau seems distant with concern. It was a blustery day; the wind was pulling at their clothes. With utter anxiety they walk noticing their surroundings. Elsie notices the shagbark hickory and loblolly trees more and how the bulbous clouds in the sky are moving. There are dogs barking and children laughing, playing in their yards. He breaks through his cynicism for once, "Yeah, we gotta give the faith healer a chance."

When they arrived they saw Pastor Charles on his porch. On Sundays he wore suits. Most other days he wore dress shirts under his sweaters. He liked wearing layers in case he got hot. He had a dry yet witty sense of humor. "Couldn't wait fer Sunday to see muh pirty face eh?" He laughed and his double chin jiggled.

He looks at their faces and realizes there is something wrong. He stands up and says, "Come on in, have a seat."

Esau stammers, "Um—we, um. "We ain't here just for a visit pastor, we need prayer." Esau was caught off guard by a framed picture on the small table of the preacher and his late wife. She had a dark olive colored tone and he couldn't tell what ethnicity she was.

Elsie puts her foot on the wooden steps of the porch and shows pastor Charles her knee. "See this here spot?" She points at it, "Used to be a seed wart, turned into cancer." She put her skirt back down. The church didn't allow women to wear pants.

"Well let me get my oil so I can pray. I feel the power of the anointin' on me right now." Pastor Charles goes into his home and comes back out with a bottle of olive oil. "This one's fresh, just got done fastin' and prayin' over it yesterday."

He puts his finger tip on the bottle of oil and lets out enough to dab his finger. He puts some on her forehead. "Father we come before you in Jesus name."

Instantly, Elsie feels a surge and she gets goose bumps, *"God's presence is stronger than before."*

"Oh Lord I feel the heat on my hand, I know you're doin' it right now. No more *cancer*." He hisses through his teeth after yelling the last word. "Your word says..." Pastor Charles didn't have to speak any longer. He looks down at Elsie's knee and notices the cancerous wart falls off. He begins to cry, "Oh Jesus, thank you Jesus, sweet Lord, your humble servant is grateful."

Esau's eyes water, "Pastor, please testify about this at church on Sunday."

Pastor Charles pulls out a handkerchief from his back pocket and wipes his tears. "Yes son, I will. I want you to be there so you can hear it too."

He looks at Esau and Elsie as he touches their shoulders, "I want you both to know that God gets the glor-eh. This ain't my doin' but the good Lord's. I'm grateful you come to me when you need help. I want you both to keep your eyes on Jesus no matter what." The pastor winces and touches his chest.

Elsie looks at him worried, "You okay? Can't you pray for yerself?"

Pastor Charles laughs, "naw, Elsie. It's just a little heart burn is all. We'll see you at church Sunday." Pastor Charles turns around and shuffles back inside.

The church had a steeple and bell tower. It had twenty steps leading to the double glass front doors. The bell was struck by lightning, causing a major fire.

Since they already had a tent nearby, they celebrated their small city's sesquicentennial. Pastor Charles invited the mayor, who was also the fire chief and pastor of the neighboring church. They had a hoo-tenanny following the service attracting bluegrass lovers. Pastor Charles used any opportunity to spread the gospel. The church resided in the west side of the city on the other side of the tracks. Many hometown natives liked to use the term as a double meaning to discriminate against the pastor's openness.

The organist was a middle aged woman named Lucille with a conservative look. She was playing a song and Pastor Charles sang along with a boisterous, slow vibrato.

*There's a church in the valley by the wildwood,*
*No lovelier spot in the dale;*
*No place is so dear to my childhood,*
*as the little brown church in the vale.*

*Come to the church in the wildwood,*
*Oh, come to the church in the dale,*
*No spot is so dear to my childhood,*
*as the little brown church in the vale.*

He's directing the church members as they walk in. He is jovial and waving for them to enter as he is singing, *"Oh come, come, come..."*

While at church on Sunday Pastor Charles starts off in a mousey tone. As he paces back and forth his voice gets louder and his mannerisms turn from quirky to intense. "The Lord almighty *healed* Joseph

Flink and brought him from near death. Then this past week he *healed* Elsie's knee from cancer. Now some of y'all may think people come here just for the miracles, but I say when I go fishin' the fish don't care what bait I put on that hook. Those fish get caught any which way. Jesus called me to be a fisher of men. In the Bible Jesus always healed people before he saved 'em."

Lucille is playing music as a backdrop and gets louder when he does. She has her shoes off for agility while playing the bass part with her feet. Many take pleasure in sitting close to watch how skillful she is. She seldom looks down at her feet and hands. Spread across her face is a wide toothy grin.

Pastor Charles hops down from the pulpit and engages his excited crowd, "I wanna get personal with you."

An elderly woman says, "Amen, Pastor tells us."

"You may ask, was God tryin' to bait 'em in? I say you betcha. I don't go to the market and buy ready-made fish."

"No you don't. Say that," A female member fans herself with her handkerchief looking around with affirmation, satisfied with what her preacher is preaching.

"That'd be like lookin' for people already goin' to church. I go out into the world and fish for people." He starts wiping the sweat from his brow with a small towel and drinks water from his glass.

"Take your time Pastor, good word." A young man from the crowd stands up and waves his arm confirming again then sits back down.

"I go where the sinners are, show 'em the Lord's glor-eh." He begins to weep with a heartbroken cry, "It's about the souls. I'll pray in the restaurant, I'll pray at the hospital; I'll pray at the grocery store, I ain't ashamed of the gospel of Jesus Christ." He's crying with earnest sincerity. "And I ain't gonna stop prayin' till the Lord takes me home. He's all I got, He's all I know. Since I was a lil' boy He always..." Pastor Charles turns his head. He sucks through his teeth the *s* sound, "Yes Jesus, you've always shown yourself real to me."

Men and women lift their hands. Many are weeping along with the pastor. Ann has a lump in her throat and swallows hard. She taught herself not to get emotional. When Ann decided she no longer wanted to feel terror her emotions decided not to feel anything else either. Her father desiccated her tears but her heavenly Father replenished them that day. She breathed in a long breath and caught by a sudden surprise...a deluge of tears roll down her face, *"It's you. I know it's you. I always feel you with me. I know what that pastor is talking about. Stay with me, please."*

Pastor Charles waves his Bible in the air, "I live because of this book. I eat, breath, sleep, and awaken with this book. Everything in here is real and powerful if you just believe it, if you just live it. I know you talk to God and he listens. But if you wanna hear him talk back to you, read his book." He shakes the Bible in the air, "Everything you have ever wanted to hear a person say to you is in this book. You may have been neglected or abused in your life and told you were good for nothin'...or maybe not told at all. Open up this book and it'll fill your heart, it will cleanse your mind, it will heal your spirit."

Ann's tears cannot stop flowing and she decides in her mind, *"If all that's true I'm gonna go read it for myself."*

Pastor Charles is inspired hops on one foot as if he received a direct line from heaven and says, "I gotta say this." He scans the crowd with his eyes, "When you truly live what's in here you stop followin' the signs and wonders, the signs and wonders start followin' you."

"Go ahead brother, preach," An excited parishioner echoes from the crowd.

"Oh son, I haven't gotten into the Word yet. A preacher ain't a preacher without the Word."

In a rapid fire like a machine gun, the pastor starts to quote scriptures one after the other with remarkable accuracy. His church is thrilled the reciting is coming from his heart.

The small church is overcrowded with people and many *"amen's"* resound throughout the sanctuary. The men sat on one side. The women sat on the other. Women wore their hair in buns as not to cause any men to lust after them. Their skirts were long as were their sleeves. The men all combed their hair to one side or straight back and were clean shaven. Pastor Charles congregation was a controversial assortment of races.

"The world likes to reject the Word," He continues to pace. Lucille is keeping up.

By now the congregation is on its feet praising, waving and cheering on their Pastor as he continues quoting scriptures pertaining to the sermon. Nurse Wiley is sitting in the front row in her usual church clothes. She wears her nurse's hat to be identified as medical personnel in case anyone needed immediate assistance. It was her first time on medical patrol at the church. It was customary for the church to have at least one nurse on call lest anyone should become ill, faint or overcome by the Spirit. The hospital was low on patients. No overtime meant she didn't have to miss church. Nurse Wiley's faith believed it was the streak of healings occurring. Doctors believed it was a coincidence.

"They reject the Word because then they won't have to believe it. You can't deny it when it's already written." He wipes his brow, "You can't deny it when it's already done. You *can't tell* a sick person who gets healed there's no such thing as healing. They got nothin' left but to praise him. God's Word says..."

Lucille follows his phrases with her interpretation of the sermon.

Although Esau never stood with the crowd, he found it gripping how well Pastor Charles knew the Bible. He aspired to be like him. It was the most zealous he'd been, enough to cause him to read his Bible religiously.

For two consecutive years Esau and Elsie experienced a normal quiet life until word came from a neighbor. Elsie hears a knock and opens the door, rubs her pregnant belly ready to give birth to child number nine. "Yeah, can I help ya?"

"Elsie, I'm sorry to tell you this but Pastor Charles passed away in his sleep last night. He's gone to be with his sweet wife Tulah and the good Lord."

Elsie puts her hand on her mouth with devastation and says, "Oh Jesus help us."

"We'll let you know when the services are held. Don't worry about bringing food to the dinner, we have it organized already. There's plenty. The committee would like for Sadie to sing a solo, Pastor Charles favorite, *"I shall see your face."*

"Thanks for the news. If there's anythin' else I can do. I'm sure Sadie would love to sing, I'll let her know."

She turns around and begins to cry full of grief and pregnancy hormones, "Esau, if it's a boy I wanna name him Charles." She didn't like to cry but all these things affected her.

Esau nods yes. He turns his head so Elsie doesn't see him weep.

During the ceremony Sadie walks up to the flimsy old music stand, adjusts it to a comfortable level and clears her throat. Lucille starts the introduction and signals for Sadie's cue to start. Sadie closes her eyes and holds on to the stand. The acoustics of the room carry her voice all around the building.

*Awesome and mighty, O Lord my Savior;*
*Giveth thou o'er and o'er to me;*
*Mercies and kindness;*
*Thou has been faithful*
*Vast is thy truthfulness forever seen*
*Vast is thy truthfulness forever seen.*

*Dew of the meadows. Shadows of trees.*
*All shown like thy presence, inside of me*
*Thy hands cradle fowl. Thy footstool, the sea*
*To thy kingdom in heaven; my soul has been freed*
*To thy kingdom in heaven; my soul has been freed.*

*Knowest my folly and taken my shame.*
*Terrible art thou in Thy holy place*
*Deliverance, forgiveness, heavens sing praise.*
*Thy shadow a refuge. I shall see your face*
*Thy shadow a refuge. I shall see your face.*

As Sadie repeats the hymn with a heartfelt resonance, she touches everyone.

Esau is numb looking at Pastor Charles' casket. A framed picture is above it. The associate Pastor, James, stands at the pulpit and says, "Pastor Charles was an amazing man who did mighty exploits for the kingdom...but the body in there is a mere corpse. This is a homecoming. He is gone to the sweet by and by." He points towards the sky as is overcome with sentiment.

Lucille, the organist, wipes her eyes.

Esau gets up to leave. He doesn't want to cry anymore. He feels drained as he waits in the car to take his family to the dinner.

The whole family is at the dinner after the burial. Esau skipped the dinner. He no longer wanted to be around these people. Elsie noticed he left in a hurry.

The children are distracted by the other member's children playing outside.

Lucille the organist says, "Elsie, Esau asked me to take you home before he left. He didn't say where he was going." She rubs Elsie's shoulder, "I have the church van, there is enough room don't worry."

Esau goes to the store for beer, leaving everyone behind. He puts his big box of beer on the backseat and heads for an abandoned road. He hurries to put the car in park to start self-medicating.

"I'm good for a long time. I finally meet a man better than my father could ever dream of bein' and God, you take him like this. He was still young." Esau is already half way done with his first can. "I don't wanna think anymore. Why should I try?"

After moving away to another home with baby Charles and the other eight children, Esau and Elsie return to their old ways. In trying to deal with the grief of losing his minister, Esau's binge got him hooked again. His stifled anger made him abusive.

Feeling dead on the inside, Elsie gave up on any notion of a good marriage. She went through the motions of life and argued with Esau as if it were normal. She gave up hope he would ever change. She became despondent and any poignant reminders of happiness were far gone. Each argument escalated beyond the next until once again, Esau causes Elsie to lose another baby.

# Chapter 14

# *Tomboy*

"Did she lose the baby?" Ann slapped a mosquito from her leg and scratched. Her blonde hair was in a long, straight pony tail. Freckles dotted her face. Her hollow green eyes were filled with stark sadness. She wipes the sweat from her forehead with the back of her wrist, looking for a place to dry it; she smears it on her t-shirt.

"She doesn't look pregnant anymore." Evan kicks a stone.

Ann gasps for a breath and puts her skinny hands over her mouth in horror. *"Wish I could run away."*

Evan doesn't look at Ann; he kicks a larger rock with force, it ricochets off an evergreen tree into the creek. "She didn't lose it, he killed it," His face is red and he's breathing with anger. "I don't wanna be like him when I grow up."

He rolls up the sleeves of his checkered flannel shirt supplied by the neighborhood church. The temperature had increased since morning. He wore jeans because of his skinny legged complex. He throws a flat rock sideways and watches it skip across the creek three times until it disappears. "I won't let him kill her." Evan looks around, "Feels good to be out here, we need a hobby or something." He wanted a distraction, something to make him forget.

George takes off running. He's charging leaning forward ready to target anything in his way. He yells, "Let's not think about anything right now, these trees need to be played on. Watch this," George takes a running start towards a white birch tree. His chubby body jiggles all over as his curly brown hair is bouncing with him. He slips, falls, and pulls himself back up raising his hands way up as if to surrender and walking backwards, "I'm okay."

Evan and Ann giggle and for a moment forget their grief, they clap, "Yay."

The side of the mountain was in full spring mode. The conflict of a warm spring sky and the neighboring city's cold atmosphere created a moisten-laden climate. Air climbed down the slopes causing a lot of rain making the ground slick. A thunderstorm was threatening in the sky yet withholding its rain. The grandiose sound of the waterfalls from the side of the mountain was soothing to the ears. The water divided at each massive boulder cascading downward as if it were stepping down from each stone in its stream. The steady water had a *whoosh* sound and was the backdrop to all the living creatures.

George balls up his chubby fingers. They look like someone had blown into two latex gloves and rolled them up. He had a look of determination etched on his face.

Evan cups his hands around his mouth to yell over the intense waterfall and the flowing brook, "Better watch it fatty, the ground is slick. You'll fall again."

Ann slaps Evans arm, "Hey, don't call him fatty."

"Is George fat or isn't he? He waddles when he runs."

Ann grins, "He's chunky."

"Honestly Ann, he's gotta be the person mom complains about. I think he's the one who gets into the food pantry when no one is watching. Look at him and then look at us."

Much to Ann and Evan's surprise George tackles the tree and begins to climb it with a vigorous tug and shouts, "Last one to reach the top is a rotten egg."

Evan and Ann each race to the tree, "I'm faster than you Evan."

Ann springs towards the white birch tree and like the tomboy she is, she pulls herself up. "You boys are about to get beat by a girl, you watch."

Evan isn't too far behind. "Look, George is making the tree bend, let's make it sway back and forth."

"Hang on everybody let's make it rock." George had a few fuzzy adolescent hairs on his upper lip. He pretends it's a thick mustache by touching the sides of his mouth, "I think I'm man enough to make this tree bend, what you think, Ann?"

Ann is laughing and with amusement says, "Yes George, you and your facial hair will go places."

The tree is now swaying back and forth creating an exhilarating feeling.

"I got butterflies in my stomach." George laughs. "Wooey."

The tree bows down to the ground almost touching the ground. It begins making a cracking sound. Their eyes widen. Evan starts to worry, "This is a tall skinny tree, what if it breaks. Maybe we should slow down?"

"Heck no, this is fun," George jibes. "You're never too old to have fun."

"Hey George, you already have a black eye, and you're gonna get another if you don't watch it, stupid." Evan tries to lean over to smack George but he's out of reach and loses his balance.

George dodges, "I'm not stupid you're stu..."

The tree snaps over the stream sending the children towards it two hundred feet down the slope.

Evan, George and Ann collapse to the ground with a loud *thump*. The trees on the side of the mountain sent the children rolling down the side almost reaching the creek. After they see they are all okay they laugh holding their stomachs.

George is the first one to pop up, "Hey let's swing across the creek on some vines."

Ann who loves to read about nature yells, "Keep an eye out for liana vines; we can climb high with those." Ann races to the vine. "I touched it first I getta go first." The vines were eight feet above the creek. She yanks on it to make sure it's secure.

George grabs the vine from Ann, "I saw it first. This one's a nice one. He yanks on it, "If we wanna swing like Tarzan we'll prolly hafta yank the vines from the ground and tie some of these vines together."

Evan reaches in, "Here let me help you tie it to this gigantic rock. Okay, George. *Now* test it."

"Test? Who needs to test?"

George runs with the vine yelling in a typical Tarzan yodel, "UH, AH, UH, AH, UH."

He hustles with the vine off of the edge with the overflowing creek below. His legs are flailing as if he were riding a bicycle. He reaches the other side of the creek and comes swinging back. He hits a protruding ledge hard and bounces back again.

"Let go dummy or you'll hit the wall again," Evan yells, "You really *are* nuts."

"The water looks great." George yells over the noisy creek and surging waterfall. He bounces off the wall again, "ow."

He let's go and slithers down the mossy rocks rolling to the edge of the creek, ending up at the edge of the water. "Hey, what's that?"

They laugh at him.

George gets distracted and wanders off. He yells, "Hey I found something."

Evan yells back, "Get back over here before you hurt yourself."

George is jumping up and down on a sealed can. "I wonder what's in here," He yells, "It doesn't wanna open."

Frustrated he can't open the can; George reaches for a hefty rock, picks it up way over his head and smashes it down onto the can. The large tin can explodes, making a loud bang.

"Aw man." George can't believe what happened to him.

Evan and Ann rush to see what George had done this time. They stand there wide eyed not believing what they see. In unison they point and laugh.

George was covered head to toe with tar. All you could see were the whites of his eyes. "Least it didn't get in my eyes," He smiles, and now you could see his teeth.

Ann laughs, "You look like the tar doll in the Brier Rabbit story."

Evan is doubled over, "That's pirty darn funny. Hey tar head."

George is sulking, "How am I gonna get this off?"

"What are you kids doing out here?"

The children are shaken with fear.

"You boys keep playing out here while Ann and me go somewhere." Esau grabs Ann, she kicks and screams. "No, I don't wanna go with you anywhere."

George says, "Where you going?"

Esau barks at George, "Shut-up and go clean yourself off."

# Chapter 15

# *Midwife*

*S*ometime later redemption for the lost baby arrives.

"Elsie, no don't push." The midwife pulled out her measuring tape.

"I'm going to measure your fundus Mrs. Flink."

"Call me Elsie," She winces with pain, "Uh. What's a fundus?"

"It's simply our birth canal." Jennifer puts on rubber gloves so she can check Elsie, "This is to determine what the gestational age is and when you might be in labor."

"Ah." Elsie screamed, but I feel the urge."

"No, no, don't push yet, this could mean a lot of trouble for the baby."

At about 2 a.m. on Saturday morning, Elsie started having the start of labor pains. She paid no mind to it since she had several other children and tightening contractions all week. To Elsie they felt like menstrual cramps.

When her water broke, she started to panic because this was her first time using a midwife to deliver a baby. Esau called the neighbor down the road who was a midwife. About 6:30 a.m. is when the midwife, Jennifer arrived. Although young she had taken classes and also came from a line of midwives. She knew from her training and experience not to let Elsie push too soon or this could harm the baby.

Jennifer reached in her big black faux leather duffle bag again, it was also a purse. It contained a small blue book with numbers of other midwives, the hospital, a credit card, and checks of client's payments aligned in her own checkbook. She had a wallet with money and an accordion of baby pictures she had delivered since her early teens with her family along with all her medical tools she needed for delivery. She was a successful and educated midwife.

Jennifer started timing the contractions to know when the baby was coming. "Okay going to warn you, you have one coming up."

Elsie almost wished she didn't know. "It feels like bein' warned someone's gonna punch me and I gotta take it."

Jennifer smiles and looks at her watch. "Just breathe deeply and try to relax, focus on something else other than the pain. A contraction is nothing but a muscle tightening and loosening. Don't look at it as labor *pain* but a tightening and loosening of the muscle."

Elsie looks at Jennifer, "Ever had-a baby?"

"No ma'am, but when Jesus allows me to be fruitful I am prepared with a super natural, not just natural child birth."

Elsie plops her head back down, *"Is this a joke?"*

Jennifer is average height and in her thirties. She appears older because she prefers to dress in a conservative fashion. She makes her own dresses, wearing them with tights and nurses shoes. Her brown hair matches her brown eyes. She pushes up her dark rimmed glasses often; they are heavy and would slide down her nose. She's thin, not thinking much about eating because of all her medical courses at the hospital. They required a lot of reading. She was single because she didn't have time to date between work and classes.

Elsie had been holding the urge to push for a few more hours. It was now at 10 a.m., "I feel pressure in my backside now...it hurts."

Jennifer smiles, "Your lower back?"

Elsie motions with her head, "Ahem, no my backside down there."

"Anal pressure is normal. Don't push yet. You know, Elsie, Jesus reversed the curse of labor for us when he died on the cross, focus on your baby not on your pain because—well..."

"Ah." Elsie screams, *"Don't hurt that bad but I can't get 'er to shut up."*

"Oh you felt that, yeah, let's focus on you and I'll be quiet. Stay right here at the edge of the bed; keep your legs up and *wide* open on the bed posts."

A few hours went by and Jennifer would tell Elsie when to push and when to let up.

"I'll support your perineum with my hand so it doesn't tear Elsie."

"Uh, ah. What's that?"

"It's the spot between both your privates."

She was supporting her perineum, pulling and pushing. Jennifer was using counter pressure so Elsie wouldn't tear. When she felt Elsie stretching, she would tell Elsie to quit pushing.

With each contraction Jennifer would check the baby's heartbeat with a stethoscope.

Elsie's full body was heaving to give birth to her child. She was sweaty and exhausted from labor and lack of sleep. Every time Elsie had a contraction she would bury her head in Esau's flannel shirt. He stood there motionless.

The children were in the other two rooms trying not to be a bother. Some were anxious and waiting, others were distracted with their toys and games. The screams were frightening the younger children but the older ones were comforting them trying to explain what was happening in a childlike way.

One of the younger ones asks, "I know the baby is coming out today…but how did it get in there in the first place?" The older child says, "Well you know how we have a recipe to put eggs and flour together to make cookies? Well that's how babies are made. Daddy and mommy put the recipe together and now mommy is having a baby. The explanation was satisfactory to the younger. Having no more questions they proceeded to play.

The bed Elsie was having the baby on was in the middle of the living room where Elsie and Esau slept. Their home was a modest home. All the rooms had an exterior door including the kitchen, living room and one bedroom. The doors were deteriorated and needed towels put under them during wintery nights to keep warmth in and snow out. Topped off with a tin roof and plank siding, this place made a home to the expected newborn Flink in the mid 60's. It didn't matter where they lived Elsie always kept her home pristine.

Jennifer was growing tired of trying to help Elsie give birth and keeping towels fresh and sterilized and commissioned Esau for the task. In an engaging smile she says, "Mr. Flink, can you please do me an enormous favor by keeping towels fresh and sterilized for us, I would appreciate it so."

He smiles back and says, "Call me Esau, I'll be glad to do that for you." His portrayal towards Jennifer meant more to him this time than being present for his own wife. He was an attention monger; he expected an approving smile with every good deed. He performed in front of her, "Got extra towels if you need 'em."

Jennifer grins from ear to ear with a positive commendation towards Esau. He is stimulated by her thoughtfulness and stays vigilant to do as she says. She interprets his devotion as a loving father and not as the deviant he is. He doesn't take his eyes off Jennifer.

Jennifer is eager about what she sees and confirms, "You're crowning, we're about to hear and see your baby."

Suddenly the baby's head appeared and the rest of her slid right out. Jennifer grabbed the baby and Elsie leaned back right away as she was told. Jennifer put the gelatinous filmed baby on Elsie's chest. She aspirated the baby's nose and mouth.

"Is it a boy or a girl? Does it have all its fingers and toes?"

"Jennifer smiles, *she* is going to be fine, I'm performing the APGAR now." Jennifer didn't wait for Elsie to ask what that was. It means, "Appearance, Pulse, Grimace, Activity, Respiration."

Elsie is engrossed by her baby and ignores her.

Jennifer smiles, "It's an acronym I don't think you care about that right now, this baby is perfect."

Although Jennifer hadn't had a baby yet, Elsie was comforted by the knowledge, experience, and gentle demeanor of her midwife. It was difficult for her to dole out compliments. She smiled at Jennifer instead.

Jennifer waited until the umbilical cord stopped pulsing, and clamped it. "Here, Esau. You can cut it now."

Esau is repulsed but puts on an act for Jennifer, "Just cut it huh." He takes the surgical scissors and cuts, *snip*. "Well, that wasn't so hard." Jennifer patted him on the shoulder and he was bolstering with pride. He was excited by her affirmation and held the baby.

Jennifer's smile turns serious again, "I know this is going to be hard but I want you to stand up so we can deliver the placenta."

After feeling the huge relief of pressure Elsie with her curls matted to her forehead, her face red from pushing cradles her baby again. "The girl name I picked for you is Miriam." She smiles and looks up at Jennifer, "I remember seeing it in the Bible."

Jennifer looks at Elsie with much delight, *"Hmm, she used scripture to christen her baby."*

With great satisfaction in his tone Esau says, "She's just in time for the reunion in a few months. I wanna take the baby to meet my folks and some of my other family." He's rocking the baby in a caring manner looking at Jennifer. He had a way of compartmentalizing his abusive ways from his public image. "You're going to grow up to be a beautiful young lady like all your sisters." He looks at Jennifer out of the corner of his eye.

Jennifer looked at him with admiration.

# Chapter 16

# *Dog chain*

Months later the time had arrived for the Flink family reunion. Esau appeared with his family of ten to the outdoor gathering. It was at his parents sprawling backyard. His father wore a clerical collar for his main job and on the side owned a great piece of real estate he was boastful of. He was the more liberal type who liked to "party." He enjoyed doing naughty things behind closed doors. Esau saw him doing this to young girls when he was young himself.

Esau saw his father talking to a young cousin and was transported in his thoughts to the time when he saw him gawking at a young girl, trying to touch her inappropriately.

His father was telling her how grown and beautiful she was. Although he made her squirm she allowed him to hug her a little too long out of respect. He showed great pleasure with her budding breasts against his stomach. As she pulled away she felt his hands brush against her chest, he pretended it was an accident. He insisted she continue sending her beach summer vacation pictures to him.

Esau knew the difference between the pride of seeing a maturing child and the lustful flattery of a pedophile. Being a pedophile himself, yet struggling with it, sometimes he was cognizant and would refrain from his daughters for periods of time. When he was conducting himself well, it gave him the illusion he didn't have a problem. He was aware he was harming them until his indecent instincts would overpower him causing him to relapse.

He remembered one of his female cousin's say, "Everyone either has the creepy uncle or is the creepy uncle." The other one bantered with a wrinkled nose, "And if you gotta ask…" They all looked back at Esau's father in disgust yet laughing. Esau realized he had become the creepy uncle. It would be one of the last moments of heightened immoral consciousness he would recognize. His depravity sunk him into a chasm of self-gratification beyond his own family's wellbeing.

Esau snaps back to the moment as they filed in like field workers, the children started exiting the flatbed truck to attend the party.

They were always physically and emotionally stifled by Esau. He taught them to remain quiet at all times much less look at people when they had company which was rare. They were all awkward and unsocialized. Every time a relative would try to talk to one of the children or pay attention to them the children would look down to the ground or look away.

His family would be taken aback moving onto others who seemed more sociable.

Esau embarrassed by his family says, "Oh so *now* you wanna be quiet. Be nice and answer their questions."

The children, lacking skills, have anxiety over answering questions. They remain uneasy and hushed during their interrogation.

An uncle was paying attention to the oldest three standing together. Evan and Ann were looking around at all the strange relatives. Their reactions were shy being out of their element. They are fidgety and nervous. George liked attention, "Yeah we never met some of you but maybe dad will let us talk to you today."

As soon as George made the spectacular announcement of not being allowed to talk Esau is enraged and yells at the children to get something to eat, "Hurry and eat something we gotta go."

Elsie is standing there holding Miriam watching her family whittled to nothing by Esau. They fall like disgraceful dominos to one side. She knew some of Esau's family didn't like her. They bad mouthed her any chance they got. She made sure to remain standoffish with the baby in a corner. Although many would ogle over Miriam they hardly paid attention to the person holding her. Elsie never felt so invisible in all her life.

Grandma Flink leaned over to Uncle Jeff to say in a murmur, "Let me go see about the riff raff. Poor, Esau." Uncle Jeff shook his head and laughed.

Grandma Flink approaches Elsie, "Oh who's that lil' girl in the pink outfit?" She tickled the baby's stomach. She never once looked at Elsie. She wanted Elsie to know she didn't care she was standing there. "Who's that? Peak a-boo—Ah, peak-a-boo." The baby pops a saliva bubble and coo's, "That's right, you're so lovable, you get that from the Flink side." Out of sheer cruelty she played with the baby ignoring Elsie. "Grandma loves you, yes she does. Coo, coo, ah, coo, coo, sweet baby Flink, coo, coo."

Elsie thinks, *"You're cuckoo alright."*

Someone yelled, "Grandma Flink your fruit salad is the best." She turns around and walks away as if Elsie hadn't been there. *"My son deserves better."*

Aunt Tilly Flink is mature and cordial. She has silver hair that looks purple at certain angles. Her stockings are constricting unwanted bulges. They also cover her varicose veins. Her clip-on fake pearl earrings match her necklace and bracelet. She leans her cane against the table before returning and shuffles up and pats Elsie on the shoulder. She coughs and with a raspy voice from years of smoking says, "These vultures treatin' you okay?"

Elsie hangs her head and tries not to laugh, "I've always liked you, Aunt Tilly."

"Don't let 'em get to ya. They're all crazy. Cute baby." She turns around and hobbles to the food table.

Elsie overhears Aunt Tilly talk to a Flink grand-daughter. "She's a good woman and puts up with a lot from Esau. You know Esau *is* Grandma Flink's favorite and ain't nobody ever gonna be good enough. Just look at all those children she's had by him. They ain't got much but they're always clean and fed."

Elsie guides each child towards the flatbed logging truck. The smaller ones sat in the cab of the truck. The older children climbed onto the back. Ann cautioned in a whisper, "Make sure you hang on to the boards of the truck, you know dad's driving."

Esau thought it was amusing to watch the frightened children in the rear view mirror. He began gaining speed. He taunted them as he accelerated around the mountain curves making Elsie beg, "Please Esau, drive slower, the children are back there and these roads are bumpy. Some of them can fall off."

Esau laughed, "Less kids to take care of."

The older children in the back could feel their legs whip around with all the movements the truck made. They made sure to clench onto the boards as tight as they could, "Hang on guys, we're almost home," Evan said.

The more terrified they looked the more Esau tried to speed up, "Let's see how strong you kids really are. You don't wanna talk? How about screaming, I'm sure y'all can scream. Do you wanna die?"

The children were sensitive to Esau's mind games and cruelty. They knew if they showed fear, Esau would make sure to intensify what they were already feeling. Their impartial looks were becoming hard for Esau to read.

"Your kids are no fun Elsie."

Elsie bit her lip to stop herself from saying what she was thinking. As they pulled into the drive she breathes a sigh of relief, grateful they arrived unharmed. *"You're an idiot, why do I put up with you?"*

At home now Esau mulled over the failed attempt at reconnecting with his family. Reaching in one too many times into the community beer cooler, Esau begins to yell at Elsie, "Your kids are so stupid. I gotta always be tellin' them to shut up. Now they got themselves a crowd to look at 'em and they wanna stay quiet."

"They're just doin' as they're told Esau."

"You're a stupid no good idiot. You know my family thinks I coulda done better."

Elsie scoffs, "Your *family* thinks or just your spiteful mother?"

Esau threatened to back hand her, "You're mad 'cause she knows the *real* you."

"No Esau, they don't see us, all they know is the junk you tell 'em 'bout me. That's all they know."

"I don't gotta say nuthin' to 'em. They just gotta see your dumb self standin' there all quiet in a corner thinkin' you're better than everybody else."

"I stood there 'cause I know they don't like me you idiot."

"That's your problem Elsie, you always got excuses. You always wanna be right."

"I think that's your problem you self-righteous moron."

"You're learnin' you bigger words to call me huh?"

Esau walks over to the family dog, *Drum*. He takes the chain from around his neck, and shakes it in Elsie's face. "You are a female dog, you're a b..."

Elsie interrupts, "Don't talk like that front of the kids."

"You cuss all the time you hypocrite. Know what dogs need? *Dog chains.* Old Drum here is more human than you; he ain't talkin' back to me."

He jerks around and looks at all the children. "You are the stupidest group of dummies I've ever seen in my life. I mean you can't get any stupider. I tell you shut up at home and you wanna keep goin.' Then at a party they're all so happy to see your ugly faces and you stay quiet."

He lunges forward and rattles the dog chain at them. They all scuttle in separate directions trying to get to a bedroom while Esau stays outside with Elsie. Ann lingers behind out of Esau's sight yet near enough to watch for Elsie.

Esau jerks the baby out of Elsie's hands and gives her to one of the older children who wanted to remain outdoors. "Here, take Miriam inside." After watching the rest of the children disappear he comes after Elsie with the chain. He gives his reasoning behind each thrashing. "You're such a b…"

Elsie ducks the strike and it infuriates Esau. "This one's for thinkin' you're better than everyone."

Elsie feels the electrifying pain of steel on her body and screams, "Ah, stop it you idiot."

He hits her again, "Quit callin' me names and respect me as the man of this house. This one's for disrespectin' me."

With each blow Elsie protects her head and her body at the same time trying to grab the chain away from Esau. Each thrash causes her writhing body to pulsate and yells, "That really hurts Esau, stop. I'm not just gonna lie down."

He flogs her again. She feels the excruciating agony course throughout her entire frame.

"This one's for not teachin' the kids to be respectful of my family." This time he nips her face and causes an instant welt to match the ones on her body."

He has her pinned to the ground with his weight as he lashes her again, "this one's just for bein' the nasty tramp you are sleepin' with different men and havin' their baby's." He wraps the chain around her neck and starts to choke the life out of her. Elsie's eyes are bulging. "You're gonna kill me, stop," She croaks.

Ann is peaking around the corner of the house and flinching with each strike, watching her mother take a beating from her brutal father. She wants to intervene but doesn't want to get in the middle of the crossfire. She knows this silent chokehold is deadlier. She is horrified for her mother.

Esau sits up to burp some of the food and beer he had too much of and allows the chain to loosen. Ann charges in and knocks Esau off balance. In a blind rage Esau beats Ann on her arms and shoulders. "You lil' no good fer nothin' you mind your own business."Like a wrestler turning over the competition, Elsie snatches the chain and starts to lash Esau turning the tables.

She grits her teeth and breathes hard as she starts whipping Esau over and over. "I don't need a reason to whip you. You ain't a man. You beat the kids, you beat me, you call us names you're just a coward a liar and a cheater."

She whips him again, "How am I gonna have time to cheat like you always say when I'm home takin' care of *your* kids. They are *all*, Esau, all *your* kids.

You keep getting me pregnant. You're the one gone for hours." She continues with many expletives over and over. She cussed like two men at a bar brawl. "You never let me leave the house."

Elsie continues taking out all her aggressions with the dog chain until Esau gives in from the tenderness starting to set in as the alcohol wears off.

"Ouch it hurts, Elsie."

"You think it felt good when you were doin' it to me?"

"I'm goin' to my family's a while. You gotta cool off woman."

Esau staggers to his car and drives to his family's. The reunion is still going strong. This gives Esau a chance to parade his bruises and swelling...showing his family the abuse he has to endure from Elsie. He was successful in embellishing the half story he had initiated giving him enough sympathy in a few minutes to last his life time.

# Chapter 17

## *How far down is up*

Twisting her granddaughter's ponytail around her finger Grandma Novak asks, "How old are you now Ann?"

"I'm eleven."

"Well the last time you stayed with me you were seven. You got tall real fast. You're a pretty young girl." She touches her nose as if it were a button.

"Beep, beep," Ann says and laughs.

Ann reaches up to Grandma Novak's nose, Grandma says in an echoing tone, "oogah, oogah."

Ann throws her head back laughing with enjoyment.

"You remembered Ann."

She looked into Grandma's captivating bright blue eyes. They looked like clear ice cubes held up to the sky allowing the blue to shimmer through, "I remember everything Granma, always have."

Grandma Novak's heart sinks, discerning the children and her daughter were being subject to a lot of physical abuse. "Well you're a growin' young girl. I say we go down to the Piggly Wiggly and get some more groceries."

"Oh, Granma, can we go to Ben Franklin's five and dime again? I wanna soda-n-ice cream, maybe some food too."

"Sure Ann. You know, your uncle Louis has a baseball game we can go watch later if you want."

"I would love to Granma." Ann trails off in thought and feels guilty for being the only sibling there.

"It's almost lunch; still want your favorite grilled cheese? You're skinny I'm sure your belly will have room at the five and dime.

Ann's eyes lit up, "With coffee and cream?" She makes a cross on her heart with her finger, "I cross my heart, hope to die, poke a needle in my eye, that I won't tell you made me coffee."

Granma Novak laughs and touches Ann's chin with her index finger and thumb. "Your eyes glow when you smile like that...makes my heart glow."

Ann smiles real big and hugs her grandma tight.

"Oh my, what's that wonderful hug for?"

"I can't believe you took the bus all the way to get me."

She strokes the top of her head, "Child I would take the bus to the moon to get you." The blue ice cubes begin melting, loosening a stream of affectionate tears. *"I have a feeling I'm not going to see you for a long time or ever again."*

Ann feels a warm sensation of love in her chest, wishing this moment would never end.

Grandma was a thinker. "You're gonna be somethin' someday." She gets up to walk towards the kitchen and looking back says, "No matter what goes on around you, you gotta know there is a road we all take in life—and that road will lead you to why you were born."

Ann looks around in marvel while waiting. Grandma Novak's rooms were packed with furniture. Most available surfaces were swarmed with knickknacks. Whenever trains would go by the ornaments would rattle because she lived near the railroad tracks. She liked to display souvenirs of places she had been and all her favorite things. The colors were vibrant rich greens and mahogany brown. The fabrics appeared richer than she was.

Grandma Novak yells from the kitchen, "The best coffee is the one you gotta grind beans for."

The intense colors made Ann feel important at grandma's house. She had the right balance of shades and texture. Grandma was savvy in adding a special touch to a room with wallpaper, stenciling and paint. Her work was meticulous.

"The secret to a good grilled sandwich is to butter the bread first," Grandma shouts from the kitchen. Ann hears the sizzling of butter melting in Grandma's iron skillet. She breathes in the scent, "mmm."

The ceilings were high and the moldings detailed. It was a two story home with a wide staircase. The siding was a sturdy wood painted white. Grandma baked a lot and liked to can fruits giving off aromas titillating the senses.

"Yum Grandma, I can taste that sandwich already."

Whenever they stepped outside they could smell the scent of freight train fuel. Engineers would sometimes throw children packs of gum when they were sitting in the grass.

Ann takes a breath so deep it lifts her shoulders, "I love all your stuff." She lets the air out.

"Rooms are meant to be filled with the people and things you love sweetheart." Grandma sets the ceramic cup and plate along with the sandwich on the coffee table in front of Ann.

"Mmm," Ann takes the first enormous bite as the cheddar cheese oozes out of the sides. The salty butter flavor is pleasing to her taste buds. With a full mouth she declares with bliss, "Oh Granma, yum." She sets the sandwich down.

She picks up the flowery ceramic plate with coffee cup and takes a sip savoring everything at the same time. The cup and plate make a light *clink* as she puts the coffee back down. With a full mouth barely understandable she says, "Nice and warm, and did you put a small block of cheese at the bottom so I can scoop it out with my finger after?"

Grandma nods *yes* with amusement. "Child you're makin' that look so good I feel like I'm eating." Grandma sets a folded napkin in front of her in a perfect triangle shape.

Ann wipes her hands on her rolled up Wrangler jeans. She's excited she might be learning to ride the men's bike grandma keeps in the garage. She didn't want her jeans to get caught in the chain. "That bike in the garage sure is nice." Her mind takes her back when she was in the garage earlier.

She liked pretending to ride the bike in the garage fantasizing about going for a spin. It was a 1941 Columbia Superb 26" men's bicycle. The color was blue and ivory. *"I can see myself riding this, honking the horn."*

She takes a sip of coffee and continues in her thought. "Ah yes, nice and hot… hope you can teach me to ride that bike later."

She loved the Torrington jeweled reflector signal pedals. It looked fancy to have the chrome rims with Columbia Superb engraved on white sidewall tires. She would sit in the authentic leather seat and look at the large pope style handlebars. She squeezed the rubber designed strips. Afterward, she outlined the brass Columbia rear nameplate with her finger, *"I can put a card in the spokes like the boys do and put my personalized nameplate below this one."* She outlined the plate with her finger when she got off the bike to go into in the house, *"I want a bike so bad."*

"We'll see Ann." *"I can't ride a bike; I hope you forget to ask."*

"Thanks." Ann moves the sandwich to the sides of her mouth creating two large bumps like a chipmunk. Ann picks up the napkin and wipes her mouth still full says, "Sorry to talk with my mouth full, but I'm enjoying this *bunches,"* Ann rolls her eyes with her statement and takes another huge bite.

Grandma Novak laughs, "I see that. Enjoy it all you want."

"Know what grandma, your right." She takes another sip to wash down what she had chewed. You're right; we all have a road to pick." Ann swallows more, "I wanna walk the roads of some places in a story book. Well actually George picked the book and we had to share." She clears the sides of her mouth with her tongue and giggles, "He only looked at the pictures and got bored with it."

Ann takes a few more bites and a few more sips while she tells her story.

"A couple a Christmases ago I was one of the last ones to reach into the poke. And I did it on purpose, ya know, cuz I knew everyone would leave the book for last."

Grandma Novak was interested and turned her body towards Ann on her antique green couch. "That was clever."

She had a quiet yet strong-willed demeanor, "What did you pull outta the sack?"

"You always taught us reading would help us do better in life—and thanks for the books you give me on my birthdays, I love reading and studying them."

"Uh-huh, yes I did Ann—and you're welcome."

"Well I pulled out a small Bible story book with pictures in it. I know this sounds crazy but I could see myself going to the places in there."

"Dreams are meant to be crazy Ann. If they were so common we'd all be doin' the same things."

"Where do you wanna go?" She smiles at Ann.

"For starters Granma, I wanna go where Jesus lived and go to the places where the stories happened. I wanna see where Jesus lived *and* where he did his miracles. I still remember the names of some of the stories, Jesus Calms the Storm, David and Goliath, and Five Little Fish. I wanna to go to Israel and then Africa."

Grandma Novak clasps her hands together in adoration and says, "Sounds like an adventure Ann. It's better than my stories on TV where everyone is havin' affairs." She chuckles.

Ann is excited someone is listening to her. She rolls up her sleeves in anticipation.

"I want you to know Ann, if you ever need to tell me anything..."

Grandma gazes at the bruises on Ann's arms and wants to cry but holds it in.

Ann looks at grandma, "When I grow up, that's another thing I'd like to do someday. I wanna help other people. I don't know how yet but I feel like I should help others. Guess I hafta figure out how to help myself," She laughs. Ann uses her hands a lot when she talks. She tucks one hand into the other when she puts them back down and shrugs.

Grandma takes Ann's head and holds her ear to her heart, "If you ever hafta run or escape, or protect yourself, don't be afraid to."

"I know, Granma."

"One day you'll tell your story."

"We're never allowed to talk Granma. We ain't allowed to tell no one nothin' or look at folk when they come over. Or look out the windows."

"I know child, but what I mean is you'll be a voice to many-many people one day."

"A lot of things didn't make sense when I was your age. Many things I went through helped the folks at my company store. They'd come in down in the dumps and I'd tell 'em a story 'bout the same things I went through and it seemed to cheer 'em up. It's like they felt normal if someone else went through the same things."

Ann points, "What's that on the coffee table Granma?"

"Oh that's my dip. You wanna try?" She asks with a mischievous grin.

"Sure. Says here *Honey bee snuff*." Ann opens the container, "Looks like cocoa."

"Well you're s'posed to dip it with a stick then brush it on your gums. Best not to tell your mom and dad...or my pastor," She chuckles.

"I think if mommy and daddy have a problem with coffee, this might be worse, let's try it," She laughs.

"We'll try it later," grandma says, let's walk to the bus station.

Ann looks at her and smiles. *"She must not want me to learn to ride the bike or maybe she doesn't know how to ride herself."*

They enjoy the scenic view on the way to the station. Walking parallel to the railroad tracks for one mile was thrilling. The earth quaking train passed by pressing out air, *"This is neat."* The expansion of steam pushed the pistons to release smoke from the locomotive. They both catch a quick glimpse of the engineer. The trains' horn roared in one pitch and lowered as each car dashed by.

Ann yells above the blare, "Oh Granma I love the bus and how we get to stand and hang on to those handles, I'm tall enough now." She pretends to grab onto the bus handle with one hand up in the air.

Grandma cups her ear, "Huh? It's too loud." You can sit in the seat with me, or stand, you're tall enough now."

"Huh, Granma?" Ann mouths to her grandma, *"I can't hear you."*

Grandma signals with her hand up and mouths, *"wait for the train."*

Ann is distracted by the rowdy train so she forgets about the snuff *this time.* The metal wheels emit sparks and send Ann into profound daydream.

*"Maybe I'll ride the train someday to go places, hmm, better yet, I'll fly. I'll prolly get there faster. What will I do when I grow up? How will I pay to get to those places?*

The train's caboose goes by. Ann looks over at Grandma for a couple seconds, clears her throat keeping her eyes on the road straight ahead.

"Yes, Ann. You can tell me anything."

"Granma, how far down is up?"

"How do you mean, Ann?"

"How bad do things gotta get," She motions with one of her hands to an invisible bottom rung. "From down here, before they get up here and get better?"

"That's a deep thought. Sometimes, Ann we all gotta make that move on our own, cuz no one will do it for us. As grownups we think we know what's best for our kids." She looks over at Ann blinking. As she mulls over Ann's question.

"So you mean sometimes you gotta save yourself? How can grownups keep stayin' in things that aren't good for 'em?"

Ann grew quiet.

"You okay, Ann?"

"Yeah, Granma. Thinkin' is all."

After some thought grandma says, "Well sometimes people live in a warm room that keeps gettin' hotter-n hotter till it turns into hell." They both walk to the booth at the station. They watch the bus as it pulls up with a screech and burst of exhaust smoke.

Grandma nears the bus, "The people in the warm room don't realize it's getting hotter so they're gettin burned cuz they're used to the room."

Ann is listening while she follows grandma.

Grandma continues talking, "They don't see anything else but the four walls in that room. They don't pay attention to the door."

Ann stares at the bus a few seconds in wonder until the door folds open bringing to life grandma's story.

Grandma steps up onto the bus and pays the driver. Ann follows up the steps and down the walkway. Grandma sits in her seat, admiring Ann. *"My sweet girl, I pray God protect you. You have so much to offer."*

Ann is standing, hanging on to the bus handle smiling back at grandma, *"It always seems like she knows what I'm thinkin'. I wish mom and dad would let me stay with her."*

Ann and Grandma arrive at the Piggy Wiggly. They exit the bus hanging onto the side rails. Ann smiles at grandma Novak, "I love you so much Granma. You always know what I'm thinkin."

Ann is used to going to the neighborhood company store; it was for the people who lived high up in the mountains. It had limited supplies brought from the city. She's in awe by the aisles of food and other things.

She looks around, "Do they call this a *super* market cuz it's so big?" She smelled the assortment of food mixed in the air. *Sniff.*

"That's right, Ann."

Ann was tempted to grab cans from the bottom of a pyramid to see if it would collapse but knew better. She loved the checkered floor and pretended to play hopscotch all the way down the aisle while grandma got the groceries she needed. Grandma is shuffling through her fanned out coupons like playing cards and checking off her list. "Granma, I wanna ride the edge of the cart backwards while you push." Ann climbs on facing grandma.

"Hang on, Ann." Grandma picks up speed and finds herself running down the aisle. "Faster Granma, faster."

Grandma is laughing and almost bumps into another patron right before she makes a screeching stop, "Err."

Ann yells with laughter, "You're so funny Granma."

"Okay, Ann, save your strength for Ben Franklin's. You're gonna need it to eat that soda float."

# Chapter 18

# *Panic attack*

C lick, clank, *crash,* silverware clashing in the background, multiple voices talking all at once, food, candy and ice cream aromas permeate the air. Ann says, "Oh Granma, this is paradise." She takes in the scents and sounds, "mmm."

*Ding ding*, a bell chimes. "Table 14 is ready." A waitress hurries and with dexterity puts one plate on each of her forearms almost tucking them in like footballs. She picks up two more plates with finesse.

Black and white photos are on the walls of people who used to go there many years before. The big signs read, *Soda Fountain, Luncheonette, Candy and more...*

The store looked like it was frozen in time since 1948 when the store opened. Ann takes a running leap onto a bar stool almost like leap frog. "I don't wanna booth, Granma. I wanna sit up here with the grownups." 1940's music is playing on the historic jukebox in the background. Ann swings her feet to the duet, *"No you can't yes I can."*

Flat round silver containers with large glass covers were displaying cookies, fudge nut brownies, and different types of breads. "I want one-a those, and one-a those, and one of those to take home, and some kinda ice cream for now."

"See, Ann? I knew you'd have room in your belly."

Ann looks up at the huge menu where the cooks and waitresses would slide the white letters and numbers into the brown slots. *Today's Special; Eggs, fried or poached omelet. Pancakes, French toast w/Bacon. Malts .30 Floats .35 Milkshakes .20.* The menu seemed endless, starting at one end of the wall to the other with many items.

Ann puts a finger on her chin, "Hmm, I can't decide if I want a float or a milkshake."

"Well I have the answer, Ann. You order a float and I'll order a milkshake, so we can share."

"Yeah, that's it. Great idea, Granma."

She looks up at a framed article of the *Daily News* from the past. *"INVASION BEGINS Eisenhower ARMY lands in Northern France. STRONG NAVAL, AIR FORCES HIT Nazi's.*

Grandma looks at the framed article at the same time, "It wasn't long ago, although it may seem like it to you. The way this world is headed, I don't think we've seen the worst of wars."

The beautiful young waitress wearing a brown hairnet and a lacey apron sets the ice cream in front of them smiling. "Here ya, go." Ann smelled a mixture of clean flowery perfume and ice cream. She looked at her name tag *Sarah Sue.*

Sarah had wavy blonde hair slicked back in a neat a bun. It wasn't a church bun but the sexy movie star up-do, braided and interwoven. She was about twenty-five. Her black bobby pins contrasted her platinum blonde hair color. Her alluring red lipstick made her teeth appear whiter. She had an attractive body causing men to objectify her. Measurements from chest to hips were in striking proportion. She used it to her advantage to get a good tip. Ann giggled at the sight of Sarah getting an enormous tip and tucking it into her apron as she batted her lashes at the gentleman. "See ya same time tomorrow, *Earl.*"

Earl ogles her from top to bottom. "Thanks for the fresh *squeezed* lemonade, Sarah."

"Oh, Granma let's not think about wars, I got enough of that at home." Let's eat our ice cream. Ann sips her float. It leaves some froth on her nose.

Grandma giggles and wipes Ann's nose with a large white cloth napkin.

Ann doesn't realize the giddiness of the ice cream makes her declare an astounding confession. Ann is too taken in by her surroundings. She looks at the malt mixer which was institutional green from the 1940's. Large steel coffee urns are close to the mixers. She watches a waiter take a soda pop glass, pump in syrup by hand, place it under a fountain and mix the seltzer with a spoon creating what most bought in cans. The waiter is wearing what appeared to be a lab coat with a white starched button shirt and a colorful blue tie. He looks young, perhaps eighteen years of age and has black hair. He's dapper and smiles with the straightest beautiful teeth she has ever seen. He winks at Ann, making her blush.

Ann wanted to feel pleasure from his wink but was conflicted on the inside. She was afraid for no apparent reason. She cleared her throat and sat up in her bar stool. *"I feel wobbly, I wonder if Granma can see me wobbly. Gosh it's hot in here all of the sudden. Why do I feel like I wanna pass out? Feels like my chest is getting tighter and tighter."*

"Are you okay Ann?"

"Umm, yeah Granma, *ahem* this is the best, ready to trade?"

Grandma looks up at the red cat clock. The eyes move side to side along with the second hand and its tail. "We need to head out soon, Louis' game is about to begin."

*"Oh good, she didn't notice. What in the world is that awful feeling? It's getting worse, it won't stop."*

Grandma recognizes Ann is having a panic attack because she used to get them when her son was in the war. She holds her hand, "You're okay Ann, you're safe with me." She rubs her back soothing her. "Do you like the ice cream? It's good isn't it?"

She knows some panic attacks are justified because of circumstances. Her cause was worrying her son would return home injured or not at all. She had saved his bike for his homecoming. When he did come back, the misfortune of his injury wasn't physical but mental and emotional. Ironically because of flashbacks and panic attacks he could not ride his bike any longer. Grandma understood Ann's reason for her panic attack was her return to her war at home.

Ann unwinds and is comforted by the cathartic warmth of her grandmother. She is stammering as she talks but doesn't realize she's stammering. She feels flush.

Grandma Novak is starting to worry. "What you're feelin' is okay Ann. When you go through a lot of things it makes you feel nervous and anxious. All you want to do is fight it. Fighting it makes it worse."

Ann widens her eyes and jerks her head trying not to pass out. "I feel like I'm gonna die, Granma what is this?" She feels her neck is shaking and she rubs it side to side.

"When you keep tryin' not to get nervous it gets worse. Keep breathing, let it happen. Invite the nervousness Ann."

"Invite it? How?"

"Ann, your nerves is your mind being afraid of fear. If you show your mind you're not afraid of getting nervous, your fear will go away and your nerves will calm."

"Okay nerves, you are welcome to come in." Ann breathes and lets whatever she is feeling play itself out.

"That's it, Ann I can see you breathing slower already. Treat it like it's a person, talk to it. Fear is God-given to help save your life from something, like a wild bear."

Ann gives a half smile, "...and there are no bears here...go ahead nerves." Ann sits up with more confidence "I'm feeling better already." Ann puts her head down in shame, "I feel foolish Granma."

"I used to get them too when your other uncle was in the war. I used to get sick of my nerves. It's just nerves Ann. You can learn to calm 'em."

Because Ann has surrendered to the fear, the panic is disarmed and weakened. In those days panic attacks and many other disorders were lumped together and called *sick of your nerves*. The room starts to come back into full focus. The cluttered sound of voices, return to random conversations. The now clear individual voices are too scattered to keep up with. Her breathing is slowing and she doesn't feel as hot.

Grandma is relieved Ann was able to conquer the panic attack. She understood when a person first learns to defuse a panic attack; it takes a few tries to eradicate them. She is trying to distract Ann, "Look at the pastries they made. I bet those would be great to take to the game later."

She knocks over a glass of water on herself purposely, "Grandma is so clumsy."

Ann starts to feel normal, "Can we get some fresh air before we leave? I feel a lot better." Ann teetered off of the bar stool.

Sarah gives Grandma Novak a fresh towel to dry herself. "Happens all the time, no worries."

Grandma Novak leaves a generous tip on the table and whispers to Sarah, "Bag me up some goodies, anything that looks good to you. I'll be back shortly."

Sarah aware Ann wasn't feeling well says, "Sure thing ma'am. She gonna be okay?"

Grandma Novak smiles and whispers, "yes."

# Chapter 19

## *Rodeo roundup*

"**I** told you I didn't want Ann or any of the kids to be gettin' ideas from your family." Esau walks in yanking on Ann's arm. They had moved to a three bedroom home in Ohio.

"It's like they come home tryin' to escape... and...I dunno, not wantin' to do as they're told." He pushes her onto the floor in revulsion discarding her. Ann gets up on all fours, stands and dashes away as if she were a hostage being freed. She rushes to her mother.

"Go to your room, Ann." Elsie motions. Ann pulls herself away from her mother and leaves.

She was still sore from Esau molesting her. Grandma's advice for her to run was met with Esau's wrath. Her hair was messed up and her clothes twisted, she hobbled to her room.

Sadie looks at Ann recognizing the signs of being molested by Esau. They both endured the abuse with ominous threats by Esau several times a week. His goal to deflower them was met with their resistance. Esau still unable, was persistent he would be their first, and threatened to kill them each time. Sadie knew this and was determined this would be his last attempt.

Esau is incensed by Elsie's disapproving look and shoves her to the side.

Sadie looks at her mom and with her eyes says, *"Did you see Ann mommy, I told you."* She moves her head with a quick tilt in Ann's direction pointing with her chin. Sadie is proud of herself for having the courage to tell her mother what Esau was doing to her.

Elsie pushes out her chest at him and with a voice of confidence says, "You just got here you *drunk* idiot and now you're pushing me around like you *own me*?"

"I do own you, slut." Esau looks out the window. "I saw tracks in the stone driveway like a cars been here." He looks back at her fuming.

Elsie looks at him with anger and says, "You're imagining things. No one's been here. Maybe a car turned around or something. You're outta your mind."

"We been here all day and there hasn't been anyone here," Sadie confirms.

"But there's car tracks," Esau looks out the window again and points.

Elsie laughs with amazement, "I know what you're doing, you're changing the subject again, and you're makin' stuff up so you don't get caught doing what you're doing...because heck...we *all* know Esau is up to no good."

He screams with spit flying, "Well I saw tracks and I think you're hiding something. Who came to visit?

You fat lazy cow." He lowers his menacing voice, "You better not be messing," He points his finger.

"Lazy? Lazy? You don't help around here, all you do is drink your beer and run off shootin' your gun, Esau. When you walked in you said they need to *do as they're told?"* She tilts her head to one side with her hands on her hips. "Explain that one to me, Esau. You *think* I don't know. Stop tryin' to change the subject."

She points to Sadie, "You're gone for hours with the girls. I swear if you touched 'em."

Evan bellows, "Touched 'em how? What's going on here?"

"Those are..." Esau yells, "Lies," as he picks up a chair and throws it across the room. The impact of the chair makes it skid, spin like a top for a moment and fall over. I ain't never touched 'em," He yells. "Those little spits." Esau's chest heaves with anger." He goes to his shelf and grabs his gun. He charges for Elsie, "You ain't got no right sayin' lies about me so you can be mad." He raises his hand again.

The children shriek, "No."

He slams her on the chest with a gun and roars, "You're jealous. You're gettin' old an' you ain't as perky as you used to be. You're just..." He gets in her face nose to nose, *"Jealous."*

"You're an idiot Esau," She screams with her eyes watering. She swallows hard and manages not to cry.

He whips her on the side of the head. She screams with each batter, "unkh, unkh, unkh," Her head is beat side to side. "Unkh."

"Jealous people are the ones goin' around doin' stuff. You know some of these here kids aren't mine, woman."

Elsie is dazed but fuming and crying with a passionate resentment, "You never let me leave out the house..." There is saliva bubbled in her mouth but is too heated and crying to swallow, "*How can you...I mean how can you say they aren't yours.*"

Esau sees her cry, points and laughs, "Ha, gotcha."

She is angrier now because he made her cry. Elsie Flink does not like to cry. She wipes her face with one swipe, grits her teeth and slowly inches close to his face. She says with a deliberate menacing whisper, "You need to face who you are or *what* you are if anything. I'm not jealous," She says standing up to him.

"You're so stupid." He dives for Elsie, wraps his hands around her neck.

She grabs his hands trying to pry them off making a weak sound, "kuhk."

The children scream, "Stop daddy. We'll go call the police if you don't stop."

"You ain't callin' nobody," he yells. He lets go of Elsie, runs after the children. He doesn't care how big or small they are or which one he hits. He smacks them on their backs with a heavy hand. They are in excruciating pain and crying. The kids are screaming randomly, "Stop, daddy. Please. Stop hurting us. Why are you doing this? Leave us alone. Mommy, mommy." With all the crying and yelling it was difficult to tell who was saying what.

His eyes are bulging with bloodshot ferocity. The blue veins on his neck look like they're one thin layer of skin from surfacing.

George runs back inside from having left earlier to play outside. Esau and Elsie didn't notice in their heated argument, "Why's dad hitting everybody?"

Esau looks at George with an angry glare and walks towards George, takes a deep breath and yells, "what were you doin' outside. I never gave you permission. You kids ain't even s'posed to look out the windows."

George walks backwards slowly as Esau walks forward ready to smack him. He's holding up his hands and pleading, "No daddy, please." He shakes his head, "No...I won't, won't do it ag..."

Esau punches him on the arm with his knuckles full force.

George screams, "ow, ow, ow," and flinches each time.

One of the little ones cries, "Leave us alone."

Esau turns to see who it is. Before he could see he heard George run away.

"Come back here." Esau hears the bathroom door slam shut and lock. *Click.*

Esau approaches Ann's room and screams, "Get out here right now."

"Leave Ann alone," Sadie yells at Esau.

Esau is enraged and screams loud enough for Elsie to hear, "You like tellin' lies to your mom, Huh?"

*"Shoulda never told,"* Sadie looks away breathing heavy, and flinching with her arm up and dodging a blow not yet given.

"Look at me," He grabs her arm. She looks up into his eyes of terror and starts to cry, "Please."

Esau throws her to the floor. He pounds on the door and jiggles the door knob. Ann sees the door knob and whispers across the room loud enough for Evan to hear, "Go to the neighbors, and call the police. He's gonna kill us all."

Esau screams at the door, "I'm gonna shoot your mommy, and y'all are gonna watch."

Elsie yells, "Don't open that door kids."

Esau grabs Elsie by the back of the neck. He pushes her to the floor, puts his knees on her back and pins her down by the neck and yells, "Die."

Esau cocks the gun. Elsie yells, "No." She reaches around to try to grab it from him. He pulls the trigger. *Click.*

Elsie flinches, *"Am I still alive?"* The hammer got caught between her thumb and index finger.

Evan, having snuck out of the room, pounces on Esau with an extension cord he found. "Help me y'all. We're not gonna let you kill her."

Ann and Sadie find the adrenaline fueled strength to help Evan.

Evan grabs Esau's hands and feet as if he were a small calf in a rodeo. "Hurry Ann, wrap the cord around his hands."

The last few beers Esau chugged down before walking in were starting to take effect, making him weak.

"You're not gonna hurt any of us anymore," Ann yells as she wraps the extension cord around his wrists and hands.

Esau squirms trying to escape. Evan puts his weight on him with his elbows, "Oh no you don't."

"Yeah," Sadie approaches with a cord she found and wraps his ankles and feet. "No more you creep." She always felt sorry for him no matter what state he was in. She started feeling guilty. *"Maybe we shouldn't be treating him like this."*

Elsie gathers strength to stand on her feet. She stands up and staggers to the door. Her French twist is loose and hanging from the side of her head. Her ears are ringing and her face is bruised with small ridges. Contusions are forming all over her body. The pistol blows to her body made her ribs sore. She's yet to discover more as the days progress.

Police sirens approach the house. Red and blue lights are rotating around a quarter mile radius illuminating their home. George had escaped out of the bathroom window to the neighbors to call for help with their phone.

Elsie opens the front door with the gun down at her side. The police draw their guns on her, "Throw your weapon down lady or we'll shoot." Unaware of the situation the police are yelling at Elsie who is holding the gun.

Elsie is battered, and bruised; she throws the gun to the ground and raises her hands, "My husband is inside hog tied. He almost killed me and my kids."

The police lower their weapons. They are now sympathizing with Elsie as the victim and not the perpetrator. They walk in and see the chaotic room and the people in it in shambles. The children are still recouping from the attack.

Evan, Ann and Sadie have their knees on Esau like a county fair prize. Esau is drooling on himself moaning, cussing, and slurring hateful things at them for tying him up.

The police are amused at the vigilante bunch protecting their own by tying up their father. The officers replace the extension cords with handcuffs and hoist Esau to his feet. They lead him to the patrol car, his face turning red then blue in the flashing lights.

George yells, "You're not gonna hurt us anymore." The others shout their agreement.

Elsie sighs with relief and tells them, "I gotta clean you-ins up first then myself. We can all relax now. Let's clean this mess."

They gather themselves and start to clean. Sadie, in the most beautiful singing voice sings, "Yes, Jesus loves me, yes Jesus loves me." She smiles, and looks at the others, "Yes Jesus loves me for the Bible tells me so."

Elsie is astonished yet pleased Sadie can sing. The sweet vibrato at the end of each measure Sadie sang was a soothing balm to Elsie's tattered soul. She doesn't say anything to Sadie because she was never used to receiving compliments. She figures they all have to learn to live without them like she did.

Sadie strokes the loose hairs on Elsie's head into place. "Don't worry mommy, we'll all take care of each other. Everything is gonna be okay now."

Elsie changes her posture, "That's enough cryin' fer now let's play." She takes an old handkerchief, wipes her face and blows her nose.

With the room and children now clean Elsie chimes, "Let's play checkers."

Evan runs to the closet, "I'll get the checkerboard. I wanna be black"

George has big a bruise on his arm and it's swollen. He bumps it on a chair from raising his hand, "ow," George says, "I wanna be red."

Elsie seemed as tough and dismissive as Esau but managed to distract them.

Ann says, "I play winner." She helps Evan with the winning move. George lets out a loud complaint, "Mom, Ann helped Evan, that's not right. She just wanted in faster."

"Nope, I'm better than you. You're mad cuz you got beat by a girl."

George lets out a curse word.

"Watch that potty mouth, George."

"But, mommy you say it all the time."

"Yeah, I'm grown up, I'm allowed."

"I can't wait to grow up so I can cuss," He folds his arms and sulks in a corner.

Elsie couldn't help but laugh at how right he was, "Your turn, Ann. See if you can beat Evan."

After a few moves Ann complains, "C'mon, Evan move your back row, you can't be there all day."

Evan makes his move and loses in moments to Ann, "You made me move my back row when I wasn't ready. Ain't fair."

"Life ain't fair, Evan," Elsie says, "Your turn, Sadie. Winner gets to pick the next game."

"Okay y'all line up." Sadie points to where she wants them to stand. They are excited for the next game. "Simon says, touch your nose. Now touch your toes." Sadie sees them all touching their nose with one finger and their toes with the other looking up at her. She says with a hysterical laugh, "I can't believe you all lost the first round."

They complain at the same time talking over one another, "But you said, Simon says touch your nose then touch your toes."

"Right, Simon didn't say to touch your toes, only your nose."

Evan dismisses her, "You cheated."

"What? You're mad you didn't win sore loser."

"I'm not a sore loser; I just wanna make sure we play by the rules."

"And the rules are whatever *Simons says*. We *do*. And whatever *we say* to do, we *don't*. Every action has to have Simon's approval."

"Oh alright, it's my turn this time, I'm Simon." Evan walks to the front of the room where they are lined up for the game and faces the lineup.

It's almost dark now and they hear a knock at the door. Elsie says, "I'll get it."

*Knock, knock, knock,* Three quick wraps on the door again and the muffled voice outside says, "Anybody home?"

Elsie limps to the door, opens it and is shocked when she sees who it is, "Yeah, can I help you?" Her heart pounds.

The police officer takes off his hat; he was one of the ones who arrested Esau. He sees the bruises on Elsie and can't imagine ever laying one hand on his own wife. He feels great empathy for her and hesitates when he breaks the news. "Ma'am we, uh, we, um, we are releasing Esau back to his, uh home, he slept off the booze." The officer sees the terror in Elsie's eyes and looks past his shoulder to the police car where Esau is in the back seat in hand cuffs.

"Oh my lord but he beat us like farm animals, he near killed me. If my hand hadn't caught that hammer you'd be doing a police report on murder."

"Sorry ma'am." The officer wishes he could keep Esau in custody. "Ma'am I tried telling the chief what happened and how y'all look and what you went through. I'm sorry but the chief said to let him go it's not our problem since you didn't press charges."

"Well geez, I thought it was obvious he beat us so bad, I figured you'd put him away for a good long while...at least to protect us. I didn't think I had to press charges."

Evan turns to George, Ann and Sadie and whispers, "Oh no, he's *really* gonna be mad now."

George is wide eyed, "Yeah, y'all tied him up, *now* what are we gonna do?" He points at himself with his thumb, "And I'm the one who called the police."

Sadie starts to worry, "He's gonna hurt us worse Ann."

Ann's eyes start to water, not from crying but from looking straight ahead and not blinking from shock. She starts to feel a panic attack coming on, *"I'm gonna go inside a room and stay close to the others. I'll lock the door and be safe."*

Elsie turns around and the rest follow, hurrying to their rooms, "That's right kids, stay in your rooms tonight; lock your doors."

"Okay, officer you can bring him in I guess."

# Chapter 20

# *Hog*

*A* *few months later the Flinks moved into a rental home on a farm.*

Bosco was a german shepherd weighing about 95 lbs. He was the family pet. Esau picked him for protection. Like the sheep protecting herder Bosco was bread for he was their guard dog. Bosco's face had a long muzzle, black nose and brown medium-sized eyes. He had a long neck he raised with excitement and lowered in a predatory fashion to prove he could hunt. His pointy triangular ears were erect and ready to listen for prey. His teeth were razor sharp like jagged leveled scissors.

Esau pets him, "Yeah, Bosco, you're a *man's* dog. Thatta boy. Good boy."

Bosco's tongue hung in delight as his master rewarded him with a biscuit and accolades.

"You look like one of them show dogs."

Esau rubbed the tan and black fur saddled around his back vigorously. He treated his family like dogs but Bosco had a calming effect on him, he liked to treat him like family, "Good boy, gotta go to work now."

The farm the Flinks were living on had a hog barn next to the house. They were not allowed access to the barn. The kids were ornery at times and the boys liked taunting the large hogs. The equipment in the barn was irresistible, so the boys would sneak in around the edges and pretend to ride in the seats. The farmer kept his equipment there on his rural property but lived in a suburban neighborhood.

In his forgetfulness Butch left the barn gate ajar. He loved taunting the hogs. He made loud grunting noises and liked poking them with large branches. "Pig, you dumb pig...*oink, oink*."

He didn't realize he forgot to latch the gate. The angry hog pushed the gate open charging at Butch. One of the other children cried out, "Oh no, he's loose."

The others thought it was funny but they were scared at the same time. Butch had been taunting the hog long enough to irritate it

To make sure no other hogs got loose, Ann runs to shut and lock the gate. "We better go inside before mom and dad find out we let a hog loose."

Joseph was worried, "What about..."

He didn't have to finish his sentence when they turned around they saw Bosco sprinting forcefully. As the hog almost catches up to Butch, Bosco came leaping through the air like a muscular show dog with a jawbone tight death grip on the hog's neck. He clamped on growling, shaking his head side to side.

The hog shrieked, twitching with large violent movements. When the spasm started to dwindle, he stopped struggling and became lifeless between Bosco's iron-like jowls.

The children were staring aghast at the hog being mauled in front of them.

Bosco opened his mouth and released the hog. He studied the animal he killed to save his family. After a few sniffs he turned around uninterested and proceeded to drink water from his bowl.

They began looking around not knowing what to do next.

Elsie heard the terrible squawk and ran outside in time to see the aftermath. She is scared the landlord will find out. "That dog is so mean." With her hands on her head she asks, "What should I do?"

Esau was away at work. Elsie was more afraid of the repercussions from Esau than the landlord.

She was terrified because she knows those hogs are worth the price of a used car. She saw how much money the farmer put into raising and housing the pig to raise it to an approximate size of 250-300 lbs. It was one of only a few big ones which made it possible for a missing pig to stand out. She takes the apron she's wearing off her waist and balls it up. "Gotta call my friend who has a pickup truck. See if we can figure *somethin'* out."

Elsie called to the children, "Y'all run inside and stay in your rooms. You done a bad thing, now I gotta fix it before your dad gets home."

Elsie looks at the dead hog, motionless with blood oozing out of its neck. "The landlord is gonna raise our rent or kick us out because of this hog. I need to get rid of it." Elsie goes inside, picks up the phone and dials, "I'm glad you're home, I need your help...Yeah Bosco killed one of the hogs... I know, it's crazy... okay I'll be waiting."

Elsie walks to Bosco's house, "C'mere boy, gonna hafta tie you up till I fix this."

Bosco is unaware as to why he is being tied up. He wags his tail at Elsie and sits after he's been tethered to his little red dog house matching the barn.

Charlotte pulls up in her black GM truck. She gets out of the truck, looks at the hog. "My sweet Jesus that thing weighs a ton. Be nice to have a hog roast. We could have everyone over but we'd be found out."

"You grab the pig's front feet and I'll grab the back," Elsie says.

They both heave to pull the hog but it doesn't move much. "For Pete's sake, let's push the darn thing till no one can see it," Charlotte suggests.

They begin to laugh at the ridiculousness of what they are doing. They smile at each other. Elsie feels a friendship with Charlotte she's never had before and wishes this moment would continue. It's a closeness she knows Esau will be threatened by. "You know not to..."

"Yeah, Elsie I got ya. I know not to tell..."

"I wish I could have you over more often. I enjoy your company Charlotte, but you know Esau." Elsie loves Charlotte like a sister which makes her miss Jackie. She feels even more secluded since most of her relatives stayed behind in Virginia.

"Best friends ain't always gotta explain, Elsie we just gotta be there for one another."

They both get behind the hog and roll it out of sight.

Charlotte looks at Elsie, "If we take my truck it's announcin' to the world we're havin' us a hog roast." She smiles, "Let's make sure to put a big tarp over it, we'll drive it down near the crick on Dolly Road to hide the evidence."

Charlotte is short and plump weighing well over 200 lbs. She's in her late 20's. Although smaller boned she had a generous amount of rolls proportioned all around her body she liked to call *baby fat*. Her self-deprecating joke was always, *"This is my baby fat, I've looked like this since I was a baby and I don't like to change it up much."* Her eyes are dark blue and her hair was a fuzzy textured blonde, she sometimes liked to French braid into two sections. She dressed like a farm girl in overalls.

Elsie and Charlotte met one day when Bosco got loose in the rural neighborhood. She was the only one brave enough to return him. Almost everyone in the country owned at least one dog. If someone's dog ever got loose it was common courtesy to return it to their rightful owners.

Charlotte firms her ball cap covering her frizzy hair, "Sounds like a plan to me. I think it'll be easier to push-n pull him onto the truck."

The women giggle like school girls on an adventure. "Alright Mr. Hog, it's been nice knowin' you on this earth, the way you used to snort and eat all

day. Now it's time for you to do that in crick heaven."
Elsie laughs putting her hand on her heart.

Charlotte laughs, "Is this the national anthem or
you tryin' to make him a funeral?"

Elsie playfully yanks on her braids, "Smarty
pants."

"Well lemme put down some trash bags first so we
don't get blood, as evidence, in the truck," Elsie walks
to the house and comes back with garbage bags.

Charlotte walks over to Bosco, "You did this huh?
You're a bad boy." She laughs and says, "Guess it
would be better to take hold of the hog's neck than
one of the kids'." Bosco licks her hand and wags his
tail as she scratches behind his ear. She looks around
for something. A board catches her eye, "Ah yes, a
sheet of plywood; perfect for rolling our buddy onto
the truck."

Elsie puts the trash bags down, "Let's count to
three." Charlotte runs over to help, dragging the plywood. She lays it against the tailgate, making a ramp.
She helps to grab the hog.

"One, two, three," Elsie counted off as they rolled
the hog into the truck. Elsie says with a grunt, "Good
Lord in heaven and earth this things gonna throw our
backs out, *whew*."

Elsie stands back and notices the truck is weighing
heavy in the back. "Gosh I hope we don't get stopped
or somthin' cuz looks like we got a body in there."

Charlotte looks at her watch, runs around to the
driver's seat and opens the door, "We gotta git."

Elsie runs to the passenger's seat, "You're right,
he'll be home soon."

Elsie burst out laughing every time Charlotte hit a bump and the hog would jump up slightly revealing what was underneath the tarp with every gust of wind. She thought it was funny to see its tongue hanging from the side of its mouth as if to taunt her, "If people only knew…you should've tied that tarp better. I feel like it's sticking its tongue out at me, teasing me."

"Cars are passing by too fast to notice, Elsie. Relax, that's just your guilty conscience." Charlotte pats Elsie's shoulder, "It's just me and you, no one's gonna find out. I'm glad you're getting a good laugh out of this."

They reach Dolly Road which is a winding road near the creek with a steep hill. They pull up to the side of the road. Charlotte as she looks around opens the truck's tailgate. Elsie leaps out to help her. Charlotte is whistling the tune to *Mission Impossible*. Elsie laughs.

Charlotte lays the board down on the tailgate and begins to roll the hog. She grunts, "We'll roll him out the same way he went in. Only this time we roll him right outta the truck, and into the crick." She begins pushing the hog onto the board towards the tailgate. Blood is oozing out onto her, "I hope nobody sees this."

Elsie and Charlotte are doubled over with laughter. Charlotte says, "Quick, hide the evidence Sherlock." Elsie takes part of the tarp and begins to dab the blood off of Charlotte's shirt.

Elsie says, "I know enough about mysteries that Sherlock was a detective not a criminal."

"You sayin' we're criminals, Elsie." She laughs, "Your honor we didn't know Bosco would attack that hog like an overgrown kid at a piñata party."

They get the hog onto the rail and shove him down the steep hills edge. They watch the hog roll down.

Elsie slaps her on the arm, "C'mon, there's a car comin' down the road. We gotta go."

As they drive off you can see Charlotte waving to the rear view mirror with a sad face. She waves, "buh-bye Mr. Hog."

Elsie is laughing, "Omagosh, we're never gonna forget this day, ain't we?" She slaps her on the arm with the back of her hand.

"No ma'am, we ain't," Charlotte touches the edge of her hats bill.

"I'll cook his favorite meal, and leave him alone with his new love," Elsie laughs.

"Love? Who's that?"

"The television, he likes watching his *Bonanza* and *Gunsmoke*. He can watch John Wayne all night long too.

"He thinks he's John Wayne, huh?" Charlotte chuckles, "He sure likes carrying his gun everywhere like him."

Elsie laughs, "Yeah, Ever since we got a television he can't get enough. That ought to distract him. He don't pay attention to the story but soon as he hears shootin' he sits up, eyes open like sewer lids."

Charlotte bats her hand, "naw, who needs a plot and storyline when all you're interested in is gunfire."

Elsie laughs and shakes her head, "Tell ya, it's them shoot-em-ups."

Charlotte looks concerned for a moment, "Where's your eldest daughter, umm Sadie? I ain't seen her in days."

Elsie gets nervous and looks away, "She's just vistin' with family till she comes back home is all."

Charlotte can tell by the inflection in Elsie's voice and her body language, something isn't right. She doesn't ask.

# Chapter 21

# *Sadie & Martha*

It was the late 60's and everyone in school was wearing their skirts inches above their hemlines with thick belts. It was the era of pea jackets, bell-bottomed pants and khaki shirts. They were cheap, military style and found in thrift stores. Sadie wanted to fit it in. As soon as she got on the bus she rolled up her long pencil skirt at the waist so her hemline could also be part of the in style fashion.

She ripped the makeup bag out of her best friend's hand looking for makeup to wear on her face, "Thanks for keepin' my stash, girl." She dabbed the foundation on first and moaned as if her face were drinking its moisturizing sensation. She liked using bold black on her upper lids for the cat eyed look. Her bright blue eyes stuck out when she did that. Her hair had a small sophisticated beehive on the top and a braided bun in the back.

"You're welcome, Sadie."

She went from smearing lightning bugs at night on her clothes for their glow—to smearing grown-up cosmetics on her face for its shimmer.

She leans over to her friend, Martha Boyd, and whispers, "Are you ready to go?"

Martha is slender with bony arms and legs. She slouches with indifference making her look short. Her skin is pasty white. Her hair is black and she likes to braid two chunks of the top sides of her hair and pin them back over her long straight hair. Her hazel eyes look like whatever color she has on. She likes to dress in her own modern chic way. Instead of a shorter pea coat she'd wear the coat longer than the skirt. Instead of patented leather heels she'd wear matte black flats.

Martha whispers back, "Where are we going?"

Sadie smiles and raises her hands, "Where these thumbs lead us." Although she was spacey, forgetful, and unable to stay on task, Sadie was also fun loving spontaneous and carefree. She begins applying thick mascara with one eye widened and her upper lip tucked under her teeth.

"How are we going to do that?" Martha asks dreadfully.

Sadie puts the bristle back into the bottle momentarily, "Whoever picks us up and takes us in the direction they're goin'. Well, that's the direction we're goin'." She continues onto the other eye.

Martha pulls out a wad of bills, "I saved up like you said too, did you?"

"Yep," She's putting nude color lipstick on followed by lip gloss." She pats her duffle bag, "Told mom we had gym when she asked me about it." She proceeded to look into the compact mirror. "Thanks for holding my make-up." Sadie pulls out her rouge.

Martha watches Sadie, "You're fast doing that. Glad I do mine at home since dad left. Mom always feels guilty for running him off and lets me do what I want."

The bus stops to pick up another student. The clanging door disrupts their conversation. Martha forgets they're still on the school bus, "So when we…" she lowers her head and her voice to a whisper, "So when we get off the school bus we sneak around to the main road and leave? Is that still the plan?"

Sadie stops and looks at her with concern, "What? Now you don't wanna go? Thought you said things were bad at home."

"Well they're not as bad as yours but I get bored sometimes. I don't know I'm sort of scared."

"If we don't like it we'll come home." Sadie shrugs, puts her hands up like she always does when she thinks she has solved a mystery.

Sadie touches up the oily spots of her face with the powdered sponge from the compact. "We'll be there in a short while, get ready to rock-n-roll."

They arrive at the school bus stop. With droves of children walking into the school, Sadie and Martha blend in and blend out of the crowd—and running towards the main road to their independence.

Sadie claps, "Yes. We did it, we're here."

"I'm glad we look older than usual. I really caked on my make up like you did Sadie."

"It's no different from the other girls at school thinking they're goin' to a fashion show." Sadie starts walking backwards and holding up her thumb.

They could feel the breeze of each car zooming by as it whipped up Martha's hair in swirls and barely made Sadie's lean to one side.

"I never thought this would feel so good, you know? I mean here we are, ready to make a new life for ourselves. How do you feel about that, Martha?"

"I gotta pee."

Sadie laughs, "me too, let's just get to the next town and we'll pee or do whatever the heck else we wanna do. Deal?"

With her slow apathetic tone Martha answers, "Well if you mean *deal* as a verb it would mean distribution…"

"Geez, Martha, relax. Look there's a trucker slowing down and pulling over right now."

The trucker opened the passenger door as an open invitation. He leaned over and asked, "Howdy girls, where you headed?"

Sadie bats her lashes, "Wherever you're headed sir."

"Call me Bubba." Bubba was tall and muscular in his mid 30's. He was handsome with a rugged and unkempt short beard. His eyes were light brown. He wore a company blue collar shirt with the name tag *Bubba*, along with jeans and work boots.

"*Bubba*, that's original." Martha rolls her eyes.

Sadie elbows her with a whisper, "sh, be nice."

"I'm Sadie, this is Martha."

The front part of the truck was spacious. Sadie sat closer to the middle and Martha sat near the door. Bubba got down and closed the door after they got in. He climbed in on his side and closed the door.

"They call me Bubba cuz everyone knows I liked blowin' bubbles with those lil' round plastic things with holes in 'em. She liked Bubbles but Bubba always stuck." He pulls out two small bags from his lunch pail. "You girls hungry? Got some deer jerky."

"Dinner *and* a show," Martha wisecracks.

"What was that lil' miss?" Bubba cups his ear right before he checks his rearview mirror and shifts his truck into gear to leave.

Sadie laughs, "She's thankful you gave us dinner and shared the road."

Sadie gives Martha a serious look.

Martha looks mouths back, *okay, okay.*

Martha leans forward, "Isn't Bubba short for William?"

"What?" Martha looks at Sadie puzzled. "I'm making conversation. Ouch don't pinch me."

"It's okay, Sadie kids your age think you know a lot about life until you get out on your own. Martha, Bubba *is* short for whatever name you can imagine. I like tellin' that story to keep my imagination goin'. I drive all day and all night. It keeps my mind sharp."

There's a map right next to Bubba's leg. He looks down and points. "This rig is goin' to Kansas City to pick up a load."

He looks at the girls. "That where you're headed?"

The CB radio emits a sound, "Breaker one nine Bubba this is Scooter, what's your 10/20?"

Martha snorts with laughter.

Sadie smiles, "Um, Yes Kansas City sir."

Bubba picks up the radio, "Good to hear from you lil' buddy, my 10/20 is the Buckeye State headed to Jayhawk Country."

Martha is impressed he knows any mascots.

"Got me some front seat cargo headed same direction. Over."

Scooter answers, "What's their handle?"

Bubba gives them his CB radio, "He's askin' your CB names, push this button and talk."

Sadie giggles, "I'm *Lightning Bug*."

"Pleased to meet you, *Lightning Bug*. Scooter here."

Sadie looks at Martha as she raises one eyebrow and gestures her head *no*.

Sadie holds the CB up to Martha's face without pushing the handle. "C'mon, Martha, play along." Sadie presses the button.

"I'm uh, *Mighty Aphrodite*." She stops and leans in again, "Um, over."

Scooter chuckles, "So you're the goddess of love *and* seduction." They hear a static sound, "Over."

Bubba rips the CB from Sadie's hand and with a serious face says, "These are my nieces, I'm takin' 'em to their aunt's house. Maybe we can do coffee sometime in the future, over."

"Sure enough, Bubba careful now, don't be feelin' sorry for no strays again, over."

Sadie laughs, "That was fun wasn't it, Martha?"

"Gotta be careful with some of these men. They're lonely and they take way too kindly to young girls that are kind to them."

"Thanks, Bubba I was just being sarcastic I didn't think…"

Bubba smiles and raises his eyebrows, "Knowledge is power Martha but sometimes experience trumps knowledge." He looks at his meter. "Gotta gas up here in Anderson, you girls gotta go?"

Martha yells, "Yes we do."

After stopping for gas, stretching and looking at the knick knacks at the gas station Sadie looks at her watch. "We should be home by now."

Martha looks worried, "Past home. Mom is still at her job but she'll be home for supper anytime with leftovers from work."

"I overheard him tellin' his buddy over there he was drivin' straight through to Kansas City. Let's hang on to the same one for the ride. He seems safe."

"Let's buy some snacks so we don't have to keep taking his food, poor guy. He grew on me," Martha smiles.

They get back on the road and see the sign *Terri Haute*, and *St. Louis*, and *Columbia*. During the ride all of the conversations, stops and naps in between wore the girls down, until they saw the sign that read *Kansas City*.

They arrive in Kansas City, Bubba pulls into a gas station to fill up on diesel, "Here's your stop ladies. Be real careful."

"Bye, Bubba thank you," Both girls give Bubba a hug on each side. They take their bags and head into town on their own.

After a few days of being gone, staying at a homeless shelter Martha says, "Sadie, we ran out of money already.

"We'll get jobs, Martha."

Martha argues, "We're not old enough, we didn't think of getting fake i.d.'s or any of that."

"Most jobs don't care these days, there are so many of them, Martha."

A homeless person overhears them talking, "I got the solution for you ladies." He writes down some information. "Just meet Tom at this wall with graffiti on it on bar avenue. He'll have a job for you both, no age limit."

Sadie smiles, "See?"

Martha smiles and takes the paper; she waits for the homeless person to walk away. She gets in Sadie's face talking real fast, "Graffiti? Bar? Serious? It's probably for prostitution or selling drugs."

"Let's give him a chance, Martha."

She puts her hands on her hips. "He's already taken too many chances Sadie, that's why he's here. *We* have to go home. Who cares what our dads think but what about our moms."

"The soup kitchen doesn't open again till tonight, I'm hungry, let's go find something," Sadie grabs Martha's arm.

Martha pulls back, "I'm taking my things this time we had some things stolen before."

"Alright, I'll take mine too."

Martha suggests the truck stop since she had a good experience with Bubba and his generosity. They walk into the truck stop and sit on a stool. They order two glasses of water.

The bell on the door rings. Two men in their twenties walk in. They look at the girls sizing them up. The dark haired one picks up a menu and flexes his toned arm. "You think this is big, you should see the back of my truck." The blonde one puts his big hand on Martha's chair, "Where you girls headed? We'll take you anywhere you wanna go?"

The dark haired man puts the menu down inching closer to Sadie, "Wanna see the back of my truck?"

Sadie smiles at this handsome young man and sooner than she can say, "Sure…"

Martha grabs her arm and pulls her away quipping, "No thanks, Sir we have an appointment."

The dark haired gentlemen is raising his arms, "What? I'm just tryin' to be nice."

"And I'm trying to be mean," Martha answers with a wisecrack. "We're not goin' anywhere."

She whispers in her ear, "They could have dead bodies piled in their trucks for all we know."

Sadie whispers back, "Quit bein' so paranoid. You read too many thrillers and watch too many movies. I'm trying to get a free meal. I can't be too quiet and I can't be too loud. I gotta be just right."

"Okay, Goldie Locks what's your angle."

"You're no fun, Martha. One meal with the boys before we go?"

Martha gives in, "Okay, but don't leave with either of them you hear me? Wait for me. I have to go to the bathroom."

Sadie is flirting with both young men and looking at the menu. "I have a big appetite." She is expressing with her body her every word.

The blonde man smiles and says, "Order all you want, it's on me. I like a girl with a hearty appetite."

The jukebox was playing, *"Ooh, baby run away with me, I have all day you see, we'll live the fantasy, ooh baby run run, far far away, run, run...run with me today, we'll take a train..."*

Martha sneaks up to a payphone, she puts her finger in the other ear to drown out the song. She sticks her finger in the "O" slot of the rotary phone, takes a breath, dials and waits for the dial to come back around, "Operator can you connect me to the police department?"

The song playing in the background makes a loud train sound and the R&B singer continues with a velvety tone climbing up and down the melodic ladder, *"woo woo, can't you hear the sound of freedom..."*

While waiting for a response, Martha leans her head out to make sure Sadie is still there and watches for a few seconds.

Sadie is still smiling and nodding but ravishing the dinner rolls in front of her with an extreme amount of butter. Her mouth was too full to talk. She smiled and acknowledged each one as they vied for her attention.

Martha heard the loud male voice in the receiver and leans back into the booth, "Yes, this is an emergency."

Back in Ohio, one hour later Elsie answers the phone. She listens to a police officer, her eyes watering. "Well they found her," she says.

Elsie wanted to report Sadie missing but Esau knew she probably ran away because of him, he didn't let Elsie do it. She turned to Esau, "She ran away to Kansas City with her friend Martha. I couldn't say anything to Mrs. Boyd because I wasn't sure she was with Sadie."

Esau looks fretful at Elsie, "I'll go get them."

"I can't believe Martha's mother called us a buncha hill billies. She said my Sadie was a bad influence on *her* Martha. It takes two, ya know. Martha ain't no angel...that little rip. Sadie didn't take her against her will."

Sixteen hours later, Esau came back with Sadie and Martha. When he stopped at the gas station he called Elsie to tell told her he would drop Martha off first.

When they got back no one said anything for weeks. Esau was afraid to make the wrong move because the police were involved. Things were peaceful around the house for several days.

Because of Sadie's escapade she was put in a children's home for a short time.

# Chapter 22

# *Just stay away*

"**M**om, dad is still messin' with us. Please say something to him." Ann is pleading with Elsie.

Elsie is mopping the floor, "Just stay away from him you lil' rip."

"How can you call me that? He keeps forcing himself. You don't understand, every time you turn around he has his hand between Sadie's legs. You can't leave us alone with him anymore. What if Sadie runs away again?"

Elsie turns her back and walks away talking, "I said just stay away and he'll stop." She walks to the other side of the room and puts the mop in the bucket.

Ann yells with crankiness, "He makes Sadie rub his head, and soon as you turn around he's fondling her. He wants me to rub his head too and when I don't— Ann lowers her voice to imitate Esau. "Stroke my head, Sadie so Ann can get jealous."

"If you know how he is Ann why do you and Sadie keep getting close to him? Just stay away I said."

"But we live here; he always makes sure to catch us alone. Maw, I'm not gonna take it anymore, he's not right," Ann stomps her foot and crosses her arms, her cheeks are blotchy. "I'm feeling really bad right now, I feel hot mommy." Ann touches the side of her head. She feels dizzy and eases herself onto the couch.

"Well you're workin' yourself up so much…who ain't gonna feel sick?"

Elsie walks to over Ann and touches her burning forehead with the back of her hand. "Omagosh you're burnin'," She walks over to the medicine cabinet to get the thermometer. She shakes it and slides it under Ann's tongue. She looks at the mercury mark, "hundred n'six, that's awful high, Ann.

Ann leans over spewing a stream of projectile vomit all over the floor.

"Ann, I just mopped." She lets out an angry expletive and yells, "Run to the bathroo…"

Ann hurls again with a violent constant puking trail on her way to the restroom until she is left with dry heaves over the toilet.

"Figures. We need to take you to the hospital and find out what's goin' on. If it's not one thing it's another. I'll get your sister to clean up your mess," She shakes her head in disappointment over the tracks of vomit. She almost throws up herself from the stench but controls it.

Elsie calls Esau at work, "Yes this is an emergency can you please tell Esau Flink his daughter is really sick. He needs to come home to get her to the ER."

She bangs the phone down and scowls at Ann saying, "We can't afford an ambulance every time one-a you-ins gets sick. You ain't worth the gun powder and lead it takes to shoot your brains out."

Esau drops Elsie and Ann off at the hospital and goes back to work. Elsie let him do whatever he wanted to keep the peace. He always said he didn't like hospitals.

Ann is checked into the emergency room. Nurses come in and out of the room as they run tests. Dr. Perez, Elsie's usual pediatrician is around and gives Elsie a lot of medical details with charts and pictures. If an intellectual person would meet him they would mistake him as condescending or patronizing. Elsie didn't see him as such. She didn't mind him being easy on the eyes. He resembled a young Ricardo Montalbán she had seen in a *Life* magazine cover once. She was thankful for his attentiveness and says, "Thanks for makin' it easy to understand." She feels guilty for being hard on Ann but doesn't let her know.

He tells Elsie in a strong yet understandable young Latino accent, "I hate to do a spinal tap on a child so young but we need to check the symptoms and find a cure." Dr. Perez doesn't wear cologne because he is aware some patients can be allergic. He looked and smelled terrific. His mother used to tell him in Spanish, *Uno siempre debe de vestirse bien para que nos traten bien...always dress nice and people will treat us better.* He pulls out a chart as he explains the procedure and how he will carry it out. He promises to talk her through it.

The nurse helps Ann turn over onto her side. Ann looks at the needle on the desk. *"Oh my goodness, they're gonna put that really long needle in me?"*

Dr. Perez notices Ann's tension. "I will need you to relax and hold real still. It will only sting for a moment. If you get tense or move around too much it *will* make this worse."

"I am going to walk you through this procedure Ann." He looks up at Elsie, "Do you have any questions, Mom?"

"Can this kill her?"

"Mom, your daughter is showing serious symptoms right now. Honestly, even the smallest procedures have certain risks. Please be assured I have never lost a patient doing a lumbar puncture or spinal tap as most know it."

"Okay, Dr. I trust you with my kid."

"Now, I need you straight in a lateral position. Please pull your knees up to your chest, Ann. Good girl, yes like that, in a fetal position."

Ann is trying not to be tense or move around too much. Elsie looks worried because the needle is so long.

"I am going to prepare the lower back. I'm using a local anesthetic along the area I will be putting in the needle. I will insert it between the lumbar vertebrae which are right here."

Ann is starting to breath heavier with anxiety.

The nurse whispers, "Relax you're going to be fine." Nurse Susan is an older nurse close to retirement. She was originally from Chicago but needed a slower paced life in Ohio. She has done this job for many years and empathizes with younger children. She has a larger frame and slightly leans forward from a bad back. Her hair is dark brown and her eyes are dark blue. She wears bifocals which cause her to adjust her head to whether she needs the far or near sighted part of her glasses.

"Okay, now I am going to push the needle in slowly until it gives. Once there, it will tell me I am into the area I want, it is called the dura mater."

Ann winces, "Ouch, sorry."

"Good girl, you are doing an amazing job tolerating pain. I still have to continue pushing the needle in until I get to the second part, which is the arachnoid mater."

"Ah that really hurts, mommy."

Elsie's eyes are furrowed, "You're a big girl you can take it."

"Okay, we are right where we want to be. This will keep the drops of cerebrospinal fluid; with this we run the meningitis test. I am going to place pressure on the puncture itself while I withdraw the needle so it doesn't hurt as bad."

"Mommy, mommy that really does hurt. I felt that in my leg."

"So sorry, Ann sometimes people will feel it in their legs when we pass a nerve." The Dr. pats her on the shoulder.

"We are almost done," Elsie grips Ann's arm and let's go.

Nurse Susan walks back in after the procedure and with a Chicago accent says, "Now you should be on your stomach for another thirty minutes. Here you go, mom here are the instructions.

Elsie takes the paper, "Thank you."

"If you need me just push the nurse's button. I'll be back in to check the puncture site again for swelling or leakage. So far so good. Ann, can you wiggle your toes and move your legs for me."

Ann wiggles her toes and moves her legs.

"Good girl, you'll be home in no time. Dr. Perez is waiting on the lab work; he'll let you know the results."

The nurse puts the clipboard back in the plastic container next to the patient name and room number. "When you get home you need to remain still for the next twenty-four hours and avoid any strenuous physical activity for forty-eight hours."

Elsie rubs her pregnant abdomen. She places her hand on her lower back and twists until she hears a slight *crack*, "Ah." Her belly button is bulging under her maternity shirt. She rubs the other side of her back, she is sore from being tense throughout Ann's procedure. She calls Esau from the hospital phone. "Hey, come pick us up," She bangs the phone down and grimaces, "I feel you moving."

Ann is home now, and resting in bed. She was discharged soon after she received all the test results.

"I'm glad it wasn't meningitis but we still don't know what it is. Just stay in bed...Ow, contraction."

# Chapter 23

# *Death of a spirit*

E lsie was in the hospital having given birth to Jill Flink. The nurse is reading Elsie's chart. "You have a pretty large family, Mrs. Flink."

"Yup, this one makes eleven." Elsie says.

"As soon as your husband was able to hold the baby for a while he left. It was during your nap. He said he had to be somewhere. Is there anything I can do for you? Would you like for me to turn on the television?"

Elsie is perturbed by Esau leaving and sighs, "Sure you can turn the TV on."

"Okay, Mrs. Flink this is the control for the television and here is the nurse button." The nurse walks out of the room.

A journalist was on the news reporting a breaking story. Elsie was shocked by what had happened.

*"This is Walter Cronkite; we'll replay the clip for you right now. This was live at the time. As you may or may not know this has already taken place."*

The headline on the television read, *Live from Good Samaritan Hospital.*

Elsie sat up in her bed to listen better.

*"Senator Robert Francis Kennedy died at 1:44 a.m. today, June 6, 1968. With Senator Kennedy at the time of his death, were his wife Ethel, his sisters..."*

Elsie begins to weep, "I can't believe he's gone too. He coulda been our hope." She adored the philanthropic acts of the Kennedy family and followed their contributions to society.

The television program continues with the headline on the screen and the aide speaking, *Frank Mankiewicz, Kennedy press aide. "He was uh, forty-two years old. Thank you."* With a somber look the aide walked off the stage and the press conference was over.

Elsie was affected in a profound way. She turned the television off feeling a penetrating loss. The staff at the hospital along with surrounding patients all mirrored one another's despair. The mood was one of mourning, shock and dreariness.

The nurse is standing in the doorway, "Can I get anything for you, Elsie. Are you alright?

Elsie wipes her eyes, "I'm fine. You can bring the baby to me when you get a chance." She didn't like to cry in public.

The impressionable young nurse says, "I'll get her for you, Mrs. Flink." She looks up at the television screen, "This will probably be the greatest catastrophe of our lifetime. God help us if anything greater happens." She picks up Elsie's water container and walks away to refill it.

Elsie grabs the phone receiver, feeling homesick she dials home. She hears the phone ring but no one answers.

Ann was downstairs in bed still ailing. She hears the phone ring but is too sick to get up. She's delirious from her unknown illness and recent procedure. Although sick she is awakened by the protests she heard coming from Sadie's room upstairs. It was the weekend in the afternoon; Ann started looking for her brothers but couldn't find them. She steadied herself as she grasped the wall trying not to faint.

*"Where's everybody at?"* Ann balances herself as she goes room to room looking for her siblings. Pale and debilitated from having had the meningitis test done. She could almost see the sounds and hear the visuals. Everything is jumbled. When she looks out the window she sees the children playing. She looks down at the door knob and notices it's locked. *"Why is the door locked?"*

Trying to overcome the roar in her head, she kept trying to hear what was going on upstairs. She was afraid to confirm what was happening because she didn't want to get caught in the crossfire. *"What is that noise?"*

She heard the muffled sounds of Sadie crying and yelling while Esau was blaring back at her. The bed was pressed up against the wall. Loud kicking sounds radiated throughout the house. The stifled yells and exchanges were difficult to understand.

*"Oh no, Sadie, I hope it's not what I think it is."* Ann's eyes were burning from being sick but now are smoldering with angry tears. She is terrorized.

She puts her hands up to her ears trying not to hear anymore but is afraid he might kill Sadie. She didn't know whether to protect her own dignity or Sadie's safety. She put her hands back down to her sides. She hears the television in the muddled background. She figures Esau must have left it on.

The children are outside and Butch is doing a dance, "I really got to pee, I'm going inside."

John says, "Dad told us to stay out here."

"Yeah, you'd better listen," Joseph agrees.

Butch runs up to the door, "I don't understand why he locks us out a lot. What is he doing in there?"

Joseph reasons, "You can go in the woods can't you?"

"Oh alright, I'll be back." Butch storms off.

Ann is looking at the door and is relieved it's locked. It is no longer rattling since Butch walked away. The sounds she heard sobered her from the pain and dizziness she was experiencing.

She hears Sadie's voice yelling with fervent cries, "Stop it. I'm going to tell mom if you don't stop. No. No."

Ann hears the other children outside playing and screaming. She thought she heard someone in another room but figured it was her imagination and ignored it.

*Later in life Miriam told Ann she had seen Esau wrestling with Sadie. She didn't comprehend and was too young to verbalize it. Miriam had walked by Sadie's room when she saw them and hid in another room from fear.*

After a while the commotion upstairs stopped. A long dead pause made Ann wonder what had happened. She shuddered to think it was any of the horrifying abuses passing through her mind. Esau came down the stairs sweaty and angry.

Ann was terrified by the racket she heard and what she imagined in her head.

As soon as Esau's eyes met with Ann she backed away from the volatile man, unrecognizable as a father. She saw him as an even more dangerous perpetrator now and realized her own life was threatened. Her body language and facial expression told him what she was thinking, *"God help me you better not touch me."*

He unlocks the front door and leaves. Sadie comes downstairs tousled and crying. She runs to the kitchen forgetting Ann is still in the house.

Ann is angry for her and wants to console her but Sadie looks downcast. Ann thinks leaving her alone is best.

Sadie turns on the faucet, pours herself a glass of water. She tries to drink it with a trembling hand. Water spills over the rim of the glass. Her skin color is ashen from the trauma she has suffered. She manages to take a few drinks. She tries to compose her mussed up hair and straighten her uneven clothes. She was too eager to put it back on after it had been forced off. The buttons on her blouse were lopsided and now so is her life.

Ann hears everything in the kitchen but pretends to be asleep she doesn't want to burden Sadie, *"She may not wanna talk about it; I'm gonna pretend to sleep."*

The children are still playing outside without a care. They are blissful being outdoors. Sadie is dismayed wishing she was as carefree. As soon as she knows Esau is gone and no longer a threat, she looks to see if she can dash back upstairs. Sadie peeks into the living room before stepping out fully, *"Good, I'm glad Ann is sleeping, I don't wanna talk about it. I'll never talk about it."* She walks over to the television and notices the press coverage of the Kennedy assassination. Sadie wonders if anyone would ever notice her spirit died that day.

Ann watched Sadie walk away shoulders sagging and despondent. She pulled the blankets up over her head praying for Sadie, praying for her mother, praying for her own healing. She prayed and cried until she felt unburdened again and drifted off to sleep.

Days passed by. Sadie's smile was hijacked from her. She was a ghost of herself drifting around after her dreadful upset. Nothing and no one existed to her. She floated in and out of her body. When people talked to her she looked them in the eye yet past them ignoring what they had to say. Most conversations ended with, "Did you hear what I just said Sadie." She would force a smile, *"Of course,"* Evasiveness kept her protected. The same emotional walls put up as her safe haven, were the same walls that sheltered her into a depth of loneliness. The turn of behavior was perceived as teenage rebellion. She felt deadened and figured a corpse cannot experience fear but only fearlessness. She demonstrated this by sporadic actions. No one could reach beyond her toughness, to the softened spot in her heart. Maybe one person could...

# Chapter 24

# *Mad for you*

S adie went to school but couldn't take the suffering any longer, "Martha, you wanna run away with me?"

"So the first words out of your mouth are; *you wanna run away with me?* I noticed you didn't bother putting your makeup on. You okay?"

Sadie shrugs.

They both stand up to get off the large rectangled yellow school bus with black trim. They watch the line shrink down with each student stepping off the bus until it was their turn. They like sitting at the back of the bus. When they get out they walk towards the school. They're carrying their heavy bags overloaded with books. This time Sadie has more than books.

"I can't run, Sadie I'm not prepared. Mom is seeing another man and he's really nice, better than dad ever was with her. Things are looking up."

Martha waves at a fellow classmate and he winks at her. He turns around and keeps looking at Martha. Sadie notices.

"He's a cutie, Martha. He's still looking. Are you going steady?"

"Nope, he's a friend. He's cute but I'm not ready for that yet. With dad's shenanigans, it's hard for me to trust anyone right now. But with this boy's good looks I'll be over it soon," Martha smiles and in a quick Groucho Marx impersonation she wiggles her eyebrows.

"Speaking of men...your dad...I thought you said your mom ran him off. Did he go out on her or something?" Sadie asks.

"Well, that's what I thought. I was *angry* with her. She protected me by not telling me he used to hit her. He never did it in front of me. Now that I know that about him, it doesn't hurt as bad he never calls."

"Maybe he doesn't call because he knows you found out about him hitting your mom. Maybe he's embarrassed." Sadie puts her head down.

"Are you okay, Sadie? You seem forlorn. You didn't say a word on the bus; you looked out the window the whole time until we got to school and revealed your master plan to run away again." She brings her hands back down and slaps the sides of her hips. "So?"

Sadie gives her a disorientated look.

"You look sad, Sadie what's the matter? Is it your dad again?"

Sadie sinks her head as huge tears roll down her face. Her arms are so crossed it looks like she's hugging herself. She begins to shudder.

Students are passing by. Some are involved in their own conversations, others are looking straight ahead and a few are staring at Sadie, wondering what is wrong with her.

"Oh no, Sadie let's go around the corner to talk more. We need privacy. School can wait."

With scores of students walking and traffic increasing towards the door it makes it easier for the girls to separate and find a hiding place to talk.

Martha doesn't say a word, she signals to a location on a patch of grass next to the building. It seemed like a worn location where many other students also took solace. They sit on the bald ground against the fire brick wall out of view.

The day was hazy and gray like the mood they were both in now. The morning crickets were loud and the tweeting birds were singing on the telephone lines. At the nearby elementary school buses were dropping students off. They ran straight to the playground screaming and playing. Cars were dropping off students while buses continued to unload additional ones to the high school where they sat. The scent of coffee was emanating through the open window of the nearby teachers' lounge, they made sure not to talk too loud. The school janitor was trimming the bushes but was far enough not to notice them.

Martha is stroking Sadie's long, straight, blonde hair, "You can tell me anything, Sadie. What's wrong?"

Sadie refuses to say or do anything. She looks up blinking, facing forward.

Martha tugs Sadie's hair, "C'mon, Sadie M'lady. Is it that bad? You can't give me a sign?" Martha takes Sadie's hand and kisses it. "You're the sister I never had. It's okay if you can't say it."

Sadie leans over to bury her face in Martha's shoulder and weeps desperately. She grieves from a solemn part of her soul. She shook her head, it was too painful to recall much less articulate.

"If it's something you can't say... was it our secret you told me never to tell?" She puts her fingers on Sadie's chin to look her in the eye, "Did he finally do what he always threatened he'd do? Did he...?"

Sadie's body weakens even more and the intensity of her anguish cannot be solely expressed with tears. Before Martha could finish Sadie clenches her hands.

"It's okay, it's okay, you don't have to tell me." Martha is fuming with passion, she breathes out with a hiss, "I want to punch something." She grabs Sadie tight, "I'm mad for you, whether he followed through or not." Her voice lowers and she breaths heavy, "Everyone who is put through something painful needs someone mad for them. You're not goin' back there."

Sadie wants to let out a scream but the severe internal ache renders her physically powerless.

"I'm not letting go until I know you're okay. You're safe now. There, there."

Sadie lets out long drawn out moan.

"I understand you're too sad to be mad. Let me do it for you. I'm mad for you, girl." Martha tips Sadie's chin upward again and looks into her eyes, Sadie looks away.

"Look at me, you're not damaged goods. You are the most awesome, funny, sweet, best friend a girl could ever have and I will never forget you for the rest of my life. I'll make sure we're best friends eternally."

Sadie's bottom lip is trembling and she bites on it to try to make it stop. The blood vessels in her eyes are red and the ones around her nose are swollen. She continues listening to Martha.

"Sweet girl you have to go...you have to leave. You can't go back to that life. You have to save yourself. Don't be afraid to run from that torment. I'll go to school but you need to get to the *Guardian Angels* home. I'll go visit you later."

Sadie nods her head yes, still unable to speak. "I, I'm..."

"It's okay," Martha takes off her sweater and wipes Sadie's face. "Keep this, remember me."

They both stand up and with unspoken words they embrace for a long period of time crying dreading the possibility this will be their last meeting.

"Oh Sadie I'm so mad for you. Remember that forever and ever."

Martha reaches into her school bag. "Here, take my book of poems."

Sadie sniffles, "I can't do that," Her cry lessens to a whimper.

"Yes, and when you're feeling lonely or scared I want you to read it. Here, better yet."

Martha sits down and with a wide eyes begins to write at a fast pace. She hands the booklet back to Sadie.

The wind blew. The sky moved. The bell rang. It was time for Sadie to depart.

*I seized the reins of your chaos*
*And pulled them in tight*
*Your innocence is not lost*
*I could see it in your eyes*
*You may have given up today*
*But in you there is a fight*
*I'm mad for you, Sadie I'm mad*
*and it feels right.*

# Chapter 25

# *Making up*

*E* *sau caught Elsie crying when he went to visit his children. They had been separated for months. She was depressed over losing Sadie. He knew she was vulnerable. In trying to win her back he overcompensated like many abusers do when they want to win back their victims.*

Esau walks in the front door, puts his hands up, "Okay kids, I've got somethin' special in my shirt. Who wants to find out what it is?" The smallest children run in screaming. They liked to see their generous father when he came for visits.

Miriam screams, "It's candy, it's candy."

"We ain't done yet. Is there a Sissy and a Bug anywhere?"

Miriam giggles and raises her hand, "Sissy, that's me."

Lori four years older than Miriam reluctantly raises her hand, "Bug here."

"While you enjoy those circus peanuts, I gotta surprise for all y'all outside. Everybody gets to have fun today."

Evan asks, "Can we have candy too, or is it only for Sissy and Bug."

Like warm air rises from the ocean's surface to create a storm. Esau answers with a self-controlled riptide and gets in Evan's face, "I'm the only one who gets to call 'em Sissy and Bug you hear?"

Evan cowers back, *"shoulda known he was fakin'... jerk."*

"Now, Sissy and Bug come to the front door and cover your eyes. I'm gonna open the door and when I say *open* you look."

The older children are perplexed at their father and how generous he was acting. History had a way of rearing its head, they were glad yet standoffish.

"Open."

They both shriek. "A pony?" Lori and Miriam hug each other. Lori shows a lot more enthusiasm this time. She jumps up and down and applauds as if she saw a show. "You got us a pony, daddy?"

The girls run outside and Lori exclaims, "She's the most beautiful pony ever Daddy."

Esau is grinning ear to ear. He sees Elsie watch through her bedroom window. He could see half of her face peering through the opened curtains. She is sitting on her bed with self-pity and is depressed about her rage. She would black out with chilling behavior leaving her scared to interact with her children. She reclines on the bed and relives a horrific moment from recent days, *"I caught Lori playing with my doll. I got so mad. I remember seeing John, Joseph and Butch diggin' though the closet and Lori holdin' my doll. Why can't I remember the rest? I blinked my eyes and I got 'em pinned against the wall with my forearm holding a ball bat ready to smash Joseph's head."* Huge tears roll down Elsie's cheek.

She hears Miriam yell, "What's the pony's name?"

Depressed for days, Elsie manages to collect herself and lean over to the window so she could watch her children in hopes it will change her mood.

Esau pulls out a grocery bag and opens a bag of carrots, "Here, you can feed her these."

Esau pats Miriam's head, "I'll let you girls name her."

Elsie slithers out of bed, puts on her robe and slippers to watch the children from the screen door.

Esau smiles at her, "Brought stuff for the kids. I have to go get yours later."

Elsie is still stone faced but watching.

Lori says, "Let's name her Judy like from the Jetsons, this pony is white and has white hair like her."

"Well you girls keep playin' with the pony, me and the others are gonna go into the woods."

Esau whistles with both fingers and rounds up the rest of the children, "C'mon kids, lets shoot some guns."

The children follow Esau on a trail. When they arrive they see targets and cans set up. "We're really gonna shoot some guns?" George asks.

Evan screams, "Yeah. That's better than some pony."

"You go first, Evan. See what ya got."

The wooded area was a large ten acre patch of trees. In the winter they looked like tall brown bare branches. In the summer they were bouquets of dazzling green. They gave the best shade to protect from the sun. This time they were brown, orange, yellow and red. They gave the illusion they were on fire. The crisp sound the leaves made when Evan stepped on them was inviting because he knew deer hunting season was just around the corner. He enjoyed hunting with his father and brothers. It was one of the few times Esau wasn't raging about something.

Esau hands him the gun with the barrel down. "Here you go, son."

Evan smiles at him. *"Son?"* He aims at the target and shoots. A can goes go down with a sound. *Ding.* *"I think this is what I wanna do with my life. I wanna join the military."*

George slaps his back. "Man, you're a natural, good job." George is proud of Evan and wants to be like him.

"I gotta go to the store and get your mom her surprise. This one will be sure to cheer her up." Can't leave you alone with the guns but do what you want."

"Okay, dad." *Clunk.* George knocked over a can with a rock.

When Esau returns from the store, he backs his Jeep into the drive. He walks in with an aquarium and fish in a separate container. He set up the fish tank with the filter, heater, gravel, driftwood and decorations. He turns the television on while he works. Esau is whistling as he's assembling the aquarium.

He looks at the instructions, "Nah, I'm not waitin' a whole week to put fish in here."

Lori walks in from playing, "Oh neat, a fish tank. Mommy's always wanted one. What kind of fish are those?"

Esau looks in the container, "These are tropical fish. Got some colorful ones she likes to look at when we're at the store. Guppies, some angel fish..."

He trails off in thought as he reacts to Lori's kindness with an inappropriate gaze, *"Can't wait to get you alone. You're nice now; you'll learn to be real nice. I gotta behave for now. Gotta win Elsie back."*

He continues to assemble the tank, "This will help teach y'all some responsibility."

For a brief moment she looks at the cartoons playing on television, "Okay, daddy." she walks away with a hop in her step excited about her new pony and the fish tank.

He watches her skip away singing. *"Flintstones, meet the Flintstones..."*

After a while of preparing the fish tank Esau puts the fish in the tank prematurely. He can't wait for Elsie to see it.

"Elsie, come out here, got somethin' for ya."

Elsie comes out of her room and looks at the tank with the brilliant colored fish swimming around. Bubbles are rising to the surface. "How much did this all set you back?"

"Don't matter, you like it?"

She shrugs with indifference, "You know I always liked lookin' at 'em."

Get dressed, "Gonna take you for a drive. You need groceries too. Your fridge is empty. Maybe we can get some food at the store and eat in the car or something."

Elsie, came to life, *"Maybe it'll be different this time."*

There's a knock at the door while Elsie is getting ready. Esau opens the door and answers, "Yeah can I help you?"

A neighbor man hands Esau a *Plan of Salvation* track, "Thought I'd come by to invite y'all to church. I wrote the information on the back of that track like last time."

*"Last time?"* Esau feels heated and asks with rudeness, "You lookin' for Elsie?"

The neighbor looks confused and nervous, "No sir, thought you and her would like more reading material. She liked the last one I gave her."

"Last one huh? Well, I think we have enough of your propaganda. I don't know what y'all are pushin' at that church but we ain't buyin."

"You're not obligated or anything thought I'd show some brotherly love. I think I'll go now."

"Okay well, I'll give these little books to the kids. You can take your brotherly love with you and don't bother coming back. I know enough Bible for all of us."

The neighbor is zealous for his cause and while leaving proclaims, "I'll be praying for your family. I'll pray the Lord's hedge of protection around your home."

Esau slams the door. He throws the track in the trash.

"Hurry up, Elsie. ain't nothin' to eat here." Esau is brusque with her but doesn't want to ruin the second chance she gave him to come back.

Elsie comes out ready for her outing with Esau, "Who was at the door?"

"No one. Wrong house."

Elsie looks at the children and says, "You know the rules. Lock the door and don't let anyone in. Don't answer the phone either. And don't be lookin' out the windows."

They caution them to behave and go on their spree.

As they walked towards the car Elsie tells him, "Life would be easier if you let me learn to drive, Esau."

"You ain't gotta be nowhere without me. Don't ask again. I can take you anywhere you wanna go." They drive off.

She mistakes his control for chivalry, and half smiles.

Home alone the children start to have some fun.

"On guard. This is my sword," John had twisted the handle off of the mop and sprang towards Lori.

Lori is laughing, "You better not hit me with that stick."

"Prepare to die," John teases, "I'll squash you *Bug*."

Lori runs to the closet, when she returns she says, "And this is my weapon." She gives her version of a fencing stance. She holds the broomstick up in the air pointing at John.

"Take *that*." John strikes her stick and moves forward.

Lori steps back, "Easy, you're hitting my sword too hard *Froggy*."

"You fight like a girl, *Bug*."

"I am a girl, take *that*."

Lori gets aggressive and overcomes John, "You think you're tough, *Froggy*?"

John laughs, "Frogs *eat* Bugs."

"Ha," She charges towards him, "And th..."

John dodges the move and Lori hits the aquarium with the broom handle smashing the tank causing all the fish to be emptied out. They are flopping on the floor.

John and Lori are stunned.

Lori runs to get a bowl for the fish, "Oh my word. John, you started it."

John says, "You're the one who crashed the tank, Lori." John is trying to catch the water in a trash can. "This water is pouring out so fast. It won't stop. Oh, gosh."

"Don't step on the glass. Look, I got one," She laughs, "Darn it slipped out."

"You take the blame, John he bought me the pony, I don't want him takin' it away."

"No, you take the blame, I didn't get a pony."

Lori gets serious, "I hope mama don't go crazy again over this."

# Chapter 26

# *When innocence encounters evil*

S ometime later Lori wakes up for school surprised to see her father's car in the driveway. She was sure she heard him get ready much earlier and go to work.

Lori was a morning person. As soon as the alarm clock went off she always sprang out of bed. The others weren't as fast as she was. Ann left earlier. She had a job before and after school. They had one bathroom to share and Lori wanted to beat everyone to it. She didn't have to wear hand-me-downs. Her father had a much better paying job. She was used to nicer things than the others had grown up with.

She hears her mother downstairs preparing breakfast while listening to country music on the radio, *"You ain't been right since you been left."*

Lori had reddish brown hair and green eyes with dark speckles in them like her mother. She was chubby and cute as a baby. She was nearing puberty and starting to develop. Her body was svelte now and maturing. She was no longer the *chubby baby*. She loved to joke with her siblings and always had something to laugh about. "Okay got one for you, "Knock, knock." She is met with silence, "C'mon, knock, knock."

She giggled, "You sleepy heads. I'm running downstairs, bathroom is all yours." Lori darted to the kitchen and peeks in at her mother, "Mom I'm sorry about your fish that one time."

"You kids need to learn to respect things more. Ain't nothin' for free. You're lucky I didn't spank you harder. It's in the past, forget it."

"So when do I stop getting spanked?"

"When you stop acting up."

Trying to distract Elsie from more chastisement, she touches the side of Elsie's hair, "Your hair is pretty mommy. Why's dad's truck out there? Didn't' he go to work?"

Elsie always had trouble with compliments but collects a semi grin, "Yeah, Lori." She pats her hand and pulls away. "He did but got burned at work so he's layin' down upstairs. Go call him before you leave for school. Tell him breakfast is ready."

"I will, but first I was wondering if I can sign up for swimming lessons. The school has a summer program and we have to sign up early," She holds up a paper, "You need to sign this. It's at the public pool."

"Why you wanna swim for?"

"Somethin' fun to do, mom. I wanna be active in school and during summer too." She is imploring with her fingers clasped, "C'mon, mom I'm gettin' good grades."

"I'll think about it. Go get your dad."

"Okay, mommy. Food smells great. I love scrambled eggs and bacon."

Elsie is finishing up breakfast and brewing coffee.

Lori is skipping steps to get upstairs. She knocks on the bedroom door, "Dad, breakfast is ready," She doesn't hear a response, "Dad?" Concerned, she opens the door and finds Esau half nude, "Oh sorry," she says.

Before she can close the door he says, "Come in, and close the door, Bug."

Her heart speeds faster unsure of what his motives are.

"Come here, Lori. I want you to touch me, make me feel better. I was burned today at work."

"Touch you where? Touch you how?" She starts feeling dizzy. She's looking all around the room trying to avoid looking at him directly.

"Here," he unveils his body. "Rub this. I'll kill you if you don't do it."

Lori does as she's told and feels humiliated, *"Why is he making me do this? It's embarrassing. Will he really kill me? I'd rather die."*

Elsie leans towards the stairs, "Esau, I sent Lori to tell you the foods done. Is she up there?"

"I'll be right there, Elsie she's in her room doing something."

He whispers, "Don't stop, Lori keep going."

"But mom wants us downstairs," She begins to cry.

"I'll buy you more things."

"I don't want anything from you. I don't wanna do this." She pulls away and stands back.

Esau gets angry and it's stifling his arousal.

Lori begins to sob louder, "Mom wants us downstairs."

"Stop crying you baby."

Lori walks in reverse, "I said I don't wanna do this, it's wrong." She turns around.

"Get back here," Esau commands.

"No, I'm not touching you that way."

Elsie calls from the kitchen again, "That you, Esau you say something?"

He lowers his voice, "You'll finish me next time."

Esau hurries to zip his pants without hurting his injured leg.

"I can bring the food upstairs."

"I'll go downstairs, almost done."

Esau reaches the bottom of the stairs. "Lori got me like you told her but she needed to fix herself more before school."

Lori had gone to her room traumatized by what her father did to her. She had never seen male genitalia. *"The first man I see and it's my own dad."* She was puzzled by what happened. She felt different, confused, violated.

"She should get down here too so she can eat." Elsie is serving Esau.

Lori cried into her doubled arms, she didn't want to wake her sisters. She wished someone could hear her cry. *"What if she doesn't believe me? What if she blames me?"* She thought of the pony he bought her and the different things he tried giving them to win the family back. She understood for the first time why some didn't want Esau around. She felt apprehensive, *"I'm gonna hafta lock the door at night. What if he tries to sneak in the room? I wonder if he's done this to the other girls."*

"Lori, get down here, breakfast is ready."

Lori's only problems before were the ones in her school homework and what game she would play that day. Now she is anxious about her father. She goes to the bathroom and uses soap, rubbing her hands together as if they were soiled trying to wash off the dirty feeling. It doesn't go away. She runs hot water until her hands turn a rose red. She looks in the mirror and sees an altered version of herself. She musters the courage to walk downstairs to go to school.

"What's wrong, Lori. You look like you've been crying." Elsie doesn't ask in a caring way but in an accusatory fashion. "Your eyes are red, what's wrong?" Elsie sets down a plate with an indifferent *clank*, "Eat before you go."

Lori doesn't feel as forgiving this time, "I'm not hungry." She gets her book bag and lunch pail and walks away. She feels tainted, shamed, and miserable. *"You make me sick. Both of you."*

"See you after school," She says with apathy. She doesn't acknowledge Esau.

Elsie is confused at Lori's sudden turn around, "I can sign that paper now if you want."

Lori keeps walking with an insensitive stomp and never turns around. She keeps to herself, walks out the front door and closes it without looking back.

Elsie starts washing the dishes, "Tell you what, these girls get a certain age and they start gettin' all huffy thinkin' they're grown up or something."

Esau is sipping his coffee, "Huh, yeah."

Lori is looking out of the bus window on her way to school. She is no longer the same. She can't stop the stream of tears. She doesn't want others to see them so she turns her head away from everyone and lets them fall. She is choked up and tries to keep her body under control. For the first time in her life she stifles her movements and doesn't express herself. The vivacious Lori they all knew becomes introverted, shy and private. When innocence encounters evil, it is diminshed by the pull of its manipulation.

# Chapter 27

# *Fishing*

"You did this to me," Elsie yells at Esau while the nurse is wiping her forehead with a wet towel. "You've been in labor twenty-four hours, Elsie you're tired."

Instead of meeting Elsie with gratitude for giving him a large family he meets her with the defensiveness he's used to. "That baby ain't mine; he's that neighbor man's that talks nice to you. Salvation tracks, yeah."

"Are you drunk again, Esau?" Those people are the nicest people I've met since Pastor Charles. They're just wantin' us to go to church with them. You don't know what bein' kind is. It's why you get so jealous. Everything is always about sex with you. When people are nice it don't mean they wanna *sleep* with you."

Esau looks at the nurse, "Call me when she gets closer, I'm goin' fishin'."

"You jerk. You're gonna get me pregnant then leave me here alone."

"I'd stay if it were mine."

"Ouch, I'm feelin' the contractions but he doesn't wanna come out."

The nurse isn't sure what the truth is but she doesn't like Esau's tone. "Maybe you should get some rest, Mr. Flink."

The Dr. walked in, "That baby just doesn't want to be born." The Dr. lifts the hospital sheet and examines Elsie. "A nap will do you good, Mr. Flink; we'll call you when she's closer."

Esau picks up the children from his parent's house on the way home. *"Sadie is gone now and Elsie is always pregnant. I'm gonna see if Ann will do more for me."* He takes a 30 minute power nap and when he awakens he tells the children he's going to take them fishing.

He is preparing for their trip with eagerness taking the equipment from the garage to the car. Back and forth he went whistling, happy he was going to have his way.

The children were stuffed into the boat Esau was rowing with vigor. He had all the fishing equipment in it ready for their excursion. The river was constricted. There was a protruding tree, its branches peeping out above the water. The water was a chocolate brown and when they looked back they could see the water treading behind the boat into a large "V".

This was supposed to be a special family time for them but Ann had an instinctive feeling it was much more. She could tell by the way Esau was looking at her with desire. She wanted this to be a wonderful family moment but she kept herself guarded. She had to survive.

Ann soaks in the fresh air into her lungs. There is a moving breeze she allows to mess her hair. She ignores Esau's gaze. She hears a large bullfrog leap into the river and notices a bird fly over them. The river is narrow and winding. The sky is a bright blue. It reminded her of Sadie's eyes. *"I miss her."*

The clouds are puffs of white cotton balls. She continues looking up at the sky where she notices the different shaped animal clouds. She wanted to play that game like she always did with Sadie but didn't want to show Esau any semblance of joy on her face.

When Esau found a spot suitable for fishing, he stopped rowing the boat there. He slowly maneuvers the oars to get the boat aligned with a nearby dock. He takes hold of the wooden dock pulling the boat near. He then secures the boat with a tag line.

They get out of the boat. "Everybody take your own fishing gear, "I gotta teach Ann how to fish better."

Esau took Ann a few more yards down the river, away from the other children. He wanted to make sure they weren't seen by the others. "Why don't ya'll walk farther that way? Yeah, that's it," He points at them farther away until he can't see them anymore.

The river is creeping along. A squirrel nibbles on a nut. Ann notices all these details because every time Esau does these things she experiences a slow death. She feels obligated to take in everything around her. She notices the squirrel's tail is bushy and upright. When it hears them coming it scampers off. The rocks are diverse shapes and sizes at the river's edge. Ann wanted to play in it, amassing some of the smoother rocks for her collection. The air feels warm and soothing but she knows soon she'll be breathing it in at a fast pace trying to fight off her father. Some trees are thin while others are thick and some interweave making it difficult to tell where one starts and the other ends.

Esau found a tree and pushed her up against it. He began kissing her. She squirmed trying to avoid his kisses. He put his hand under her dress then began touching himself. Ann wanted to scream to get out of it but she knew better. He guided her hand to make her rub him. All she could do was fantasize about being somewhere else. Her disassociation kept her spirit from dying. It was one of many moments that Ann had to learn to survive.

Like many other times the scenery changed but his behavior remained the same—and every time it happened, Ann was somewhere else in her mind. This was a different fishing day of the many with the same deeds. *"I have to find a way to leave. I can't take this anymore. Poor, Sadie I wonder how she's doing. He's more demanding since Sadie is gone."*

Ann hears Joseph's discernable laugh in the distance, it takes her back to a memory. She had a recollection of her relatives coming over to pay a visit to see the newest baby, Cain Flink. They were all discussing how difficult it was for Elsie to give birth to him given it took 38 hours...and how Esau arrived in the nick of time.

Still being molested, Ann remembers the wholesomeness of her relationship with Joseph. It gives her the strength to raise her voice at Esau. It was a memory she had experienced recently. "Don't touch me. I can't stand it when you touch me. You do what you gotta do but leave me alone today."

Esau is wrapped up in himself he doesn't touch Ann and continues with his depraved fixation. He lifts her dress to look, "Least lemme look or I'll beat you."

Ann closes her eyes, reverts to her remembrance of her experience with Joseph.

*"You-ins go outside and play while we have company." Elsie points to the door. Most of the children run outside to play, including the visiting children.*

*They were excited to have their cousins over and permission to play with them. One of the children bellows, "We have a swing set out back, let's play on it. There's a huge tire tied to a tree we can swing in too."*

*"Let's go to mom and dad's room, see what we can find," Ann tells Joseph as she puts her finger on her lips, Shush."*

*"We're already outside, Ann."*

*"We'll slip through the back door. They're all in the living room, they won't notice."*

*They both tiptoe through the back and towards the bedroom. Joseph opens the door for Ann and whispers, "Ladies first."*

*Ann giggles, "Feels like a top secret mission."*

*Joseph walks in first, "You always had an imagination Ann. I know where daddy hides the 22 rifle." He walks towards the closet, pulls the gun out and hands it to Ann.*

219

*"This can't be loaded, there's no way," Ann looks at the gun with adventure and suspicion. She was aiming at different objects in the room like an expert sharpshooter. "Pow," She aims again. "Pow."*

*"Hey, Annie Oakley, why don't you shoot me," Joseph grabs the barrel of the gun and pulls it to his chest. While holding it he laughs and says, "Go ahead and shoot me."*

*"Are you kidding or just being stupid?" Ann ribs, "What the heck, it's not loaded anyway."*

*For a split second she feels a glint of fear and almost senses a tug making the gun aim towards the edge of the bed as she is pulling the trigger. Bang. The gunshot sounded like a loud firecracker.*

*The bullet going through the mattress and the bed springs jolted the two of them into reality. They both jumped and realized in an instant what could have happened.*

*"I coulda killed you, Joseph. I coulda killed you," Ann is staring at the hole in the mattress in a stupor.*

*"You almost killed me, Ann."*

*"I know. Look at the hole in the mattress. Now what? I hope they didn't hear the gunshot."*

*"What if we stuff it with a piece of cloth or something," Joseph looks for any piece of material to cover it up while his hands are still shaking. He stuffs a sock in the hole but it pokes out too far.*

*Ann balls up a piece of paper and stuffs the hole as much as she can.*

*"Let's put the gun back, hopefully they'll never notice. Don't ever tell. Don't tell on me, Ann."*

Ann is transplanted back into her current state hearing the echo of Joseph's voice turn into Esau's. "Don't tell on me, Ann."

Esau lights up his pipe. Ann gathers herself and starts walking back to where the others are. She hears screaming.

"Daddy, daddy, we don't see Evan anymore."

The children were frenzied watching Evan's head bob under water. He had taken a dive off of the dock and had gone below as the rivers current swallowed him under the surface.

As Ann ran to them she saw Evan come up then go down a second time.

Esau ran past Ann. With his pipe still in his mouth and fully clothed, he dives in after Evan. "Evan, where are you?" Esau is frantic. He is going in and out of the water looking for Evan, but can't find him. "Evan," He yells, flapping his arms to pull himself under the water with force. He has to go by feeling. The water is too muddy to see anything.

A family lives across the street on a high hill facing the mucky river. They hear Esau and the children screaming.

Evan comes back up a third time and tugs on Esau, "Ah." He exclaims. Being panicked and confused, he pulls Esau under water.

"No, Evan it's dad. I'm here to save..." *splash, gurgle.*

They both go under. There are now two people drowning.

A man from across the street runs down the steep hill and jumps in. He finds Esau first and begins to pull him from the river.

"No, not me, get the boy. I can save myself."

# Chapter 28

# *Trip to the store*

"Esau, I'm gonna need some things from the store."

"Okay, I'll take Ann with me."

Elsie has that gnawing feeling in her gut but ignores it once again. "Alright but hurry back, I already started cookin'."

"Mom, I'm not sure I wanna go."

"It's just to the store and back, Ann. I'll buy you something," Esau pleads, "Redhots? Jolly Ranchers? Your favorites."

Elsie says with an indifferent wave, "It's up to you, Ann. Make up your mind. He offered to buy candy, go for that if you want."

"Listen to your mom and get in the stupid car," Esau says with an impatient growl.

Ann walks to the car, *"We'll be in a moving car, how bad can it be."*

As Esau is backing out of the driveway, he puts his arm around Ann instead of on the car seat to look back. Ann sits forward angry over his constant passes.

"Stop touchin' me. I'm sick of you."

"Open my pants, Ann."

"I ain't openin' nothin', I'm tellin' mom."

"Do as you're told. You didn't think you'd hafta pay the piper, did ya?"

"I won't pay no stupid piper. I don't want anything from you."

Esau reaches over trying to touch her breasts. "Stop," she yells as she slaps his hand.

"You let me before, what's changed."

"I never let you; you threaten to kill me or say that mom will kill you if she found out and leave us all orphans. I hate you."

"C'mon, Ann. Lemme."

"No," She protests.

He takes a heated breath and turns red. The veins on his forehead pop out. He grips the steering wheel with such force, his knuckles turn white.

"I'm gonna *have* you tonight." He used the worldly expletive, it terrified Ann.

Esau reaches over and pulls on Ann's skirt. With a knee jerk reaction and blinded craze Ann reaches for the car handle. She opens the moving car door and throws herself out of the car. Her heart is pounding fast; the scenery is a speeding moving blur as she hits the gravel and continues to roll a few more tumbles until she comes to a stop.

He slams on the breaks, making the tires squeal. He looks at her in the rearview mirror. Esau knows she might tell her mother about this so he spins away and continues on to the store.

Ann pushes herself up to her sore knees first. She stands slowly. Her entire body aches but the adrenaline is stimulating her exit. Only a few yards from her house, Ann darted home as if she were a sprinter.

She runs into the house and is winded, taking big gulps of air.

"What are you doing back so fast, Ann?"

"I changed my mind."

Elsie watches her gasp for air. Still recouping from a fall and a fast run home, Ann stops and doubles over in trepidation. Elsie follows her gut for once, "Go to your room and lock the door."

Ann ran to her room and locked the door. *"I need a plan, what should I do."* She looks in the mirror. Her palms are on the table, her shoulders to her ears, she says, *"Think, Ann think."*

Elsie waits for Esau to come home. As soon as he walks in she asks, "What did you do to Ann?"

"What are you talking about? I didn't do anything to Ann." He walks past Elsie not looking her in the eye. "She changed her mind, didn't wanna go and jumped out of the car like an idiot. She's just like you and your stupid mother...afraid of everything."

"Well maybe you gave her something to be afraid of." Elsie folds her arms, "What did you do?"

"Don't be stupid. Is this worth getting a separation again? You know you don't like being alone."

"Well if you did something maybe it is."

"What exactly are you accusin' me of this time, Elsie? I swear you're really stupid. Go cryin' to your mama again."

"You leave my mother out of this."

The phone rings. Esau picks up, "Hello... Who is this? Jack Mastedon? Why you calling here? Wrong number, eh." He slams the phone down, *jingling the internal bell.* "Who's Jack?"

Elsie curses, "Beats me, wrong number, you heard him."

"You're lying. You're a liar just like your mother."

"Your mom is liar, Esau. She never sees us and says mean lies about me all the time."

"Don't you *dare* talk about her. *Ever.*"

Elsie puts her hands on her hips, "How you think it makes me feel when you talk about my mom."

"You think I care how you feel? Haven't you learned by now I don't give a whoop what you feel? Go back home with your stupid, no good for nothing, prying mother." He flips Elsie off...calls her the most degrading name a female can be called, "...and your mama is one too." He turns to walk away.

"Evan almost lost his life in that river and it scares you into reading your Bible again. You quote scriptures and think you're some kinda god that can do what he pleases."

"The Bible says I rule over you. You're always actin' like a harlot."

Elsie feels her body getting hotter and hotter. In an act of absolute rage she takes a sharp knife from the kitchen. She dives towards Esau and pushes him down to the floor and pins him there. She straddles his back putting her full weight on him. She grabs him by the shirt collar ready to stab him. Her knees are placed on his arms.

Ann, upstairs, hears the commotion and comes running to find Elsie ready to stab Esau with a knife. "No, mommy. You'll go to jail." Ann tries to hold Elsie's arm. She wrestles with her mother's super-human strength.

"Get your crazy mother off of me, Ann."

"What did you do to Ann? Tell me, Esau." She asked with a shout.

Elsie looked glazed over with rage still trying to stab Esau. Ann seizes the blade. She inches her way to the handle, taking the knife away with only a few nicks. "This isn't worth you getting locked up for, mom. You need to calm down."

Ann looks at Esau and tells her mother, "He's not worth you going to prison, mom." Ann restores the weapon back into a kitchen knife by placing it in the sink. She looks at her mother with great sympathy watching, Elsie trying to calm herself from the heated moment.

Esau gets up and walks out the backdoor, knowing Elsie isn't going to take any more from him.

"You better leave. You can't live here anymore." Elsie yells at the slammed door. The curtains are still waving side to side. Elsie is still on her knees when she says, "You better leave."

# Chapter 29

# *Bikes*

"**A**ren't you happy you got this job, Joseph?" Ann and Joseph are cleaning the school gymnasium. They were also in charge of cleaning the multi-purpose room and library. The school was small and under budgeted. The multi-purpose room was part of the gymnasium. It was split in two with a grey vinyl mesh divider. It was one small gymnasium divided in two for added legroom. "You look gloomy."

"I am happy, sis; I want that bike so bad but…"

"…but what?" Ann smiles, "I'm your sis, you can tell me anything."

"I don't know how to ride one."

"Me either, we've never owned a bike before. How are we gonna know how to ride one?"

"Well, I figured since you have friends at school that ride them, you already learned how."

"Nope, we're gonna learn together. I really wanna learn, Joseph. It means *more* freedom for us."

"I know…I do too. We can ride our bikes to our jobs instead of walk every day. We just need to find someone that'll take us to the store."

"How about we learn how to ride them first, then we can ride to our jobs every day."

They both laugh.

"You inspired me, Ann. Ya know, when you bought yourself some neat clothes and stuff. The way I see it if you can take care of yourself. I can do the same."

"It started off as somewhere to go besides home and something to do, but when I felt the freedom of buying what I wanted, I was hooked."

"I hate askin' dad for stuff. He always makes me feel like I'm an outsider bein' a burden."

"Don't take it personal, Joseph; he's like that with mom too."

Joseph and Ann are sweeping the gymnasium. They have long wide wooden brooms. They divided the room into two sections to work faster.

"You're really good at doing this, Joseph."

"I learn from the best."

"You're a good brother, Joseph. You're gonna make a great dad someday."

"You really think I'll be somebody, Ann? I'm not sure about that. Dad really knows how to take the wind outta people's sails."

"Then you gotta make your own wind. Just think…a few more days of walking to school and you get your first paycheck, Joseph. That ought to be enough to make you feel good about yourself."

Ann pushed the divider back and latches it. "Time to do the other side of the gymnasium."

"This is getting done fast."

"Let's see, what kinda bike do I want?" Ann stops and looks off into the distance. "I want the Schwinn Sting-Ray like the other kids here."

"I wanna dirt bike, you know more of the boy kind of bike—but I want it to be black."

"That's a great idea, Joseph. I hear the boys are using the Schwinn's to ride in the dirt over bumps and do daring tricks. I saw some girls put baskets on the front of theirs; I can put my books and stuff in my basket. I like the glittery yellow ones."

Joseph laughs, "No sissy basket for me. But you can hold my stuff if you want."

"Sure, sure, lemme carry all your stuff so you can be Mr. Tough Guy," Ann uses her best sarcasm. "It's alright I don't mind," She says with a grin.

"Push that broom or we ain't gettin' a paycheck to pay for these dreams."

Ann looks at Joseph, "Remember the time you picked on me and I beat your butt to the ground? You left me alone after that." She continues laughing.

"Yeah I do, I told the others, don't mess with her, buddy." Joseph is raising his eyebrows with assurance. "You swung me around like one of your rag dolls then threw me like *Gorgeous George* or some other big time wrestler."

"I don't know, Joseph. Sometimes he seems kinda fake."

"Yeah, but the can o' whoop you opened on me was real." They laugh.

"Do you remember the time you almost died when you were in the hospital and the preacher prayed for you?"

"I sorta remember. I think I've been told that story so many times it became a memory."

"Yep, you almost died. But because of it mom and dad started going to church for about two years. Those were almost the most perfect years of our childhood. Dad didn't hit us and...well..."

"Gosh, too bad I don't remember those years much. Maybe that's why, huh? We probably tend to remember the bad stuff over the good. Mom always said that. Just remember the good memories...that's what keeps you going."

Ann wishes she could divulge more with Joseph, *"That's cuz there was more bad than good."* She opens her mouth but hesitates, "Right, Joseph...only remember the good. Wow, time is goin' by so fast. Now we're ready to mop."

He picks up a piece of paper and makes an origami flower. "Here, this is for you." He smiles, *"I never told you about the time mom almost beat me with a baseball bat."*

Ann has a lump in her throat but forces it down. She doesn't want to show she's touched but does want to acknowledge his talent. "You've always been so good with your hands. Remember that for when you get older. Grandma always said we already know what we're gonna do when we're kids, we just gotta find a way to get paid for it as adults."

Ann and Joseph finish up their work in the gymnasium.

"On to the library now. My favorite place."

"I wish it was mine too…glad I only have to clean it," Joseph laughs.

Days later they pick up their checks. A neighbor was kind enough to drive them to the store to pick up their coveted bikes. The sign read *Peddling Bike Shop…family owned and operated over 40 years.* They walk into the store. There are racks of bikes lined up on the floor and bike racks hanging in midair. There was a sign above the register. *The best in sales, rentals and repairs in the area.*

There were different colors, shapes and sizes for men, women and children in the showroom. According to signs, the sections were, *the serious pro biker, customized & specialized, biking enthusiasts.*

Joseph points, "That's us, Ann. *Biking enthusiasts.* They have the Schwinn." Joseph looks at the tag beneath the bikes. With a lowered voice he says, *"And the price is rrright."*

Ann laughs, "Look even Captain Kangaroo likes the Schwinn bike, it's gotta be good." There is a life-size cutout of Captain Kangaroo making a *thumbs up sign* next to the bike. Joseph stands next to it with his mouth open, his thumbs up too.

Ann laughs at him, "You're so funny, Joseph."

The salesperson walks up to them. "The bike of your dreams is waiting for you to ride it. I can also help you with accessories, from helmets to shoes and bells to baskets."

Ann points to another sign. *Buy this week and get a 2 year parts warranty—free.*

The salesperson says, "Yep that's right, the same guy that custom makes the bikes fixes them too. He knows his craft."

Ann looks past the sales clerk, "I want that basket."

"I want this helmet for my daring tricks." Joseph was already wearing one.

They pay for their bikes. Joseph thanks their neighbor for the ride. He tells him with confidence they can ride their bikes home.

Joseph gets on his bike and swerves left to right and back again before he falls with the bike.

Ann laughs, "Nice try."

He picks his bike up and dares her, "You think it's easy? You try, Ann."

Ann gathers her things and puts them in her basket. She starts to pedal her bike. She gets a little farther than Joseph before she falls and the contents in her basket are emptied onto the ground.

Joseph runs with his bike to where she is, "You okay?"

Ann wipes the pebbles from her hands and knees and giggles, "Yeah, we'll get the hang of it. We can do this. We'll be pro's you'll see."

Cars are driving by Ann and Joseph. They are walking their bicycles on the side of the road believing they'll soon learn to ride.

# Chapter 30

# *Driving Lessons*

E lsie is vigilant of Ann. Whatever Esau did to Sadie to make her leave Elsie was sure he wouldn't do the same to Ann. She made sure to keep them separated no matter what. Esau grew frustrated. He would ask to take her to the store or go fishing. Every time he was met with a negative response. Often Elsie ignored his requests. After months of pondering Esau thought himself up a perfect idea. Walking in from work one day he approached Elsie.

"You have a lot of work with the kids and since Sadie is gone and Evan and George went off to the Army, you're gonna need someone to run errands for you when I'm not here. How 'bout I give Ann some drivin' lessons?"

Elsie looked up for a moment, in thought. *"They'll be in a moving car, can't be all bad."*

She looked at Esau, "Okay, but don't be gone long."

Esau was excited he got his way, "I'll start her off with the station wagon and when she gets confident I'll teach her how to drive the Jeep."

Esau yells at the bottom of the stairs, "Ann."

Ann yells from upstairs, "What?"

"Mom said you could start drivin' lessons, got the keys right here." Esau jingles the keys loud enough for her to hear.

"Hold on." Ann sits on the bed excited to be driving without a permit but conflicted because she figured she'd have to pay the piper.

"Well, you gonna come down or what?"

After a few reluctant minutes Ann makes her way downstairs.

"You-ins don't be gone long, Esau." Elsie is finishing up drying the dishes. "Dinner will be ready when you get back."

"Love ya, mom. Be back." Ann has a skip in her step but caution in her spirit.

"We'll start off with the station wagon." He hands Ann the keys and smiles.

She looks at the keys for a few seconds before taking them, "Can't believe I'm gonna be drivin'."

"Yep, we better git."

The white station wagon had brown imitation panels on both sides. It had a metal luggage rack on top for cargo. The rear gate had two handles, one for the window and the other for the entire door. Ann envisioned her younger siblings crawling through the window instead of the door. It seemed more fun to them. Although the newer models had a vinyl top this wagon was in mint condition. Esau treated his material belongings with care.

Ann got in the car. She watched her dad drive many times and emulated his moves. She adjusted the rearview mirror first. She adjusted her seat and side mirrors. She clipped in her seatbelt and put the key in the ignition.

Esau said, "Give it a little gas and she'll start for ya."

Ann started the station wagon. Esau looks down at her feet and inches closer to Ann. Ann pulls away with unwillingness.

Esau scoots back, "Keep your foot on the break then put it in drive. Try not to use two feet."

Ann is feeling butterflies in her stomach. "I'm doin' it, I'm drivin'."

She has her hands at 10 and 2 o'clock.

Esau reaches into his pocket, "I got something for you." He shows her a faux pearl necklace with matching earrings. "Let me touch you and you can have these." He tries holding her hand.

She bats him away. "I don't want it."

"But they're real pretty. Look at 'em."

"I'm not gonna do anything with you. Why you keep showing me that necklace every time you wanna do something to me. You had it for a long time. Give it to mom or something."

Angrily he says, "Turn the turn signal off stupid. It's still blinking."

After about 20 minutes of driving Esau gets restless.

"Okay, we drove enough; go down that dirt road ahead."

"Why?"

"Cuz I said so. Do it. Or you know what's good for ya."

Ann puts her turn signal on. She has a burning in the middle of her chest. Her stomach is turning and her face is full of angst. She turns into the deserted road hand over hand.

"Hurry up, Ann."

She is startled, "Just wait."

"Put it in park." Esau lets the mirror down to look at himself as if he was on a date and his hair had to be perfect.

"You know, Ann Elsie's no good. Sadie's gone. You can me my special girl." He takes off his seat belt and leans into her.

Ann is gripping the steering wheel so hard her hands ache from the tension. She doesn't want to remove the only barrier between her and her pedophile father, her seatbelt. She's looking straight ahead.

"We can get this over with fast or you can fight me, your choice." He takes her seatbelt off.

Ann is mortified and wants to scream. She wants to die and wishes he would kill her like he always threatened. *"Better to die than go through this."*

Birds fly overhead, a stray cat walks in front of the wagon. Esau is trying to stick his tongue in her mouth but she keeps pushing him away. She looks up at a vibrant green tree and notices a tiny birds nest. Esau is halfway disrobed now and she's looking away

237

as much as possible. She doesn't want to see him like this.

He proceeds to do all manner of physical and sexual harm to her.

Right before he tries to penetrate she screams, "No. No. You can't do that to me. You can't get me pregnant."

Those words jar him out of the lustful state he is in pulling him back to reality.

Ann has found the magic phrase for Esau to stop from going all the way. Many driving lessons were to follow. Again she would repeat the phrase, *"You can't get me pregnant."* It would keep Esau from fully violating her.

Her lips were swollen from Esau sucking on them. Her breasts were too, they would be tender and bruised for days since they were budding. She finished dressing, looked up at the birds nest and saw the mama bird bring back food for its nestling. Ann watched the bird while Esau put his clothes back on.

"You tell Elsie, I'll..."

"Kill you, yeah got it, dad."

His look told her, *"You better not talk back to me like that again."* He doesn't say a word to her because he is afraid she will tell on him.

Ann arrived home with her father. It was another day though they could have all run together because he did the same things on every occasion. This time was different. As soon as Esau leaves the house she goes to Elsie and says, "I don't want driving lessons anymore with dad. He keeps messin' with me and I don't want that."

"It's your fault Ann; you know what he's like."

Ann is appalled at her mother's statement. She looks at her mother with horror. *"How can you betray me like this?"* Ann frowns in disbelief, "He threatens me." She stomps.

In a flippant way Elsie says, "If you take any more lessons, your two brothers will go with you."

A few days went by and Esau decides to take Ann for lessons at night.

"Elsie, Ann and me, we're goin' to do some drivin' lessons, it's been a while."

"Not alone, the boys are goin' with y'all."

"What for? They don't need to come."

"I said the boys are goin' with y'all."

"Fine, we'll take the red Jeep."

"Joseph and Butch, y'all ride with Esau and Ann for her lessons."

Ann looks up, *"Oh thank goodness, I'm finally gonna be okay."*

Esau disappears out of the back door. He's taking shovels from the garage to the Jeep. "They think they can outsmart me." He sneers.

When the boys get their shoes on and are ready to go Esau comes back to the kitchen, "Okay everyone, in the Jeep."

The red Jeep had square fenders, a ragtop and a roll bar directly behind the front seat. It had square fenders. Esau loved four wheeling in it and because the Jeep was originally made for the military, it made him feel manly.

"Alright, Ann. Do the same things, 'cept this time you hafta learn stick."

Ann takes a mouthful of air, "So push in the clutch first then start the Jeep, right?"

"Right, you've seen me do this. Here's *reverse,*" He slides the shifter into gear to get her started."

"Slowly let the clutch out and give it gas."

Ann accidently lets the clutch out too fast. The Jeep lurches backwards and Joseph hits his head on the back of Ann's seat. Butch laughs at him.

"Quiet. Ann needs to concentrate. Try it again," Esau turns his head back from glaring at the boys.

Ann slowly pulls out of the driveway. She gets it right this time.

Esau says, "Push in the clutch and the breaks so you can stop."

"Ann, you've seen me drive. Every time you wanna shift gears push in the clutch and let off the gas."

As Ann gets going, she's grinding the gears. Esau tells her, "Keep tryin' till you get it right."

Ann feels the challenge and in the next gear she starts to drive the Jeep smoothly.

Joseph and Butch are smiling in the backseat wanting to cheer her on but are afraid to speak up.

"Go down that road up there."

Ann's heart starts to race.

"Pull over at the start of the road here."

Esau gets off the Jeep and pulls the shovels out, "Get down here boys, you're gonna do your civil duty and fill these here pot holes."

"Why do we hafta do this, dad?"

Butch repeats Joseph, "Yeah, dad why do we hafta do this?"

"You need to learn how to work," Esau gets back in the Jeep and tells Ann to drive.

Ann looks at the boys in the rearview mirror, *"So that's what he was bein' secretive about...that's why he had shovels."*

"Ann, drive to our location."

*"Our location? You're gross. I'm not your girlfriend."*

Esau opens the glove compartment. He doesn't waste time getting started because he knows the boys are down the road. He was fearful they might get curious to find out what he's been doing to Ann. He pulls out the petroleum jelly and opens the can. "You lean up over the front seat and pull everything off."

"You're gross, I don't wanna do that."

He clicks the gun he put in the glove compartment, "Did you hear that? I brought it with me."

*"I just wish you'd use it."* Ann grudgingly does as she's told. He tries pleasuring her and asks if she likes it. She doesn't say a word either way, because she's frightened and revolted.

"Are you a virgin? I can take you to the Doctor to find out—and if you're not, I'll beat you."

He finishes. He's tired of fighting and never completes his goal. He's so angry he makes her sit in the back while he drives. He picks up the boys and heads home.

The ride home is hushed. Esau is snarling as he's driving and the boys are too scared to ask any questions. The strain in the atmosphere is almost tangible. Ann is quiet trying not to show she's wiping away tears. *"God please hear me, I don't want to do this anymore.* She wipes her face, *"Please help me get through this. I know it's not your fault..."* She takes in three sobbing quiet breaths, *"I need you, God. I really need you."*

As soon as they get home she runs towards the stairs.

Elsie looks at her, "What's wrong."

"Nothing, you don't care anyway." Ann runs upstairs, slams her door and throws herself face down on her bed, her face buried in her pillow. *"I'd tell you but you always blame it on me, you won't protect me."*

She stops holding back the fountain of tears and lets loose. She finally makes a decision. *"Next time he does something..."*

# Chapter 31

# *Boating*

Esau and Elsie's marriage was a revolving door. They had been married and divorced twice now.

He didn't want to mess up again so this time he thought he'd procure for himself some redemption.

He was on the phone with one of his co-workers. "That boat I bought is a real beauty. I'm thinkin' on takin' her out on a spin with the family. The kids will love it."

Esau takes the coiled phone cord and pulls on it while he continues to talk, "Did you like the vegetables I brought to work? Oh yeah? They all said that about me? They think I have the best garden... I dunno. I like Lloyd's garden too but if they say mine is best than I guess it is."

Esau is beaming with pride. "No problem... You're welcome... There's more where that came from... Well I'm glad the guys at work think I'm a great guy."

Ann overheard the conversation. *"Great guy? Yeah, I wanna puke."*

He is still elated, "Hey, thanks for that catalogue... Uh-huh, oh yeah really? We got the same kinda boat then... That's amazin'. Okay buddy, see you at work sometime. I took a personal day today. It's too nice to work, goin' boating. I'm gonna smoke me my new pipe to celebrate my new boat." He laughs, "...Sure I'll take a few puffs for ya. Alright, bye."

Ann was determined she wasn't going to go boating. Her mother had already chosen Esau over her when confronted by a social worker. She didn't feel safe anymore.

She runs to the next room before Esau sees her and she tells her siblings. "I'm not goin' boatin,' y'all go, I ain't goin'.

Butch tells Ann, "Who do you think you are?" Butch stands up with a manly posture. He's starting to look muscular. He's arrogant and irritable.

Ann says, "Shut up, Butch you don't know why I don't wanna go."

"You don't know what he'll do to us if we don't listen," Butch goes back to a memory of when they lived in Ohio. Esau purchased a new travel trailer and allowed Butch, Joseph and John to sleep in it. When Esau entered the trailer in the morning after the boys got up he noticed one of them wet the bed. Because none of them wanted to tell on each other Esau began pulling small chunks of hair from each of their heads until one told. The bottom of the trash can was full of hair. Joseph finally fessed up.

Ann thinks, *"I do know what he'll do Butch, Joseph told me and I pretended to have to ask dad something, I peeked into the trash and saw all the hair. It made me sick to my stomach."* Ann rubs her stomach.

"Yeah? Well I don't care if you don't wanna go, but you're gonna tick him off if you don't. We all know you're his favorite," Butch says in a whiney voice.

John says, "I don't feel like getting beat today, Ann none of us do." John has blonde hair that is starting to show a tinge of red like his father. His brown eyes are intense pleading with Ann. John has a flashback of Esau coming home from his second shift job. Earlier in the day Esau told Elsie to make John and Joseph rake leaves. When Esau returned he saw his huge front lawn had not been raked. He pulled John and Joseph out of bed at 11:30 p.m. and laid them on the floor. Esau put his knee on Joseph's neck and whipped him.

John rubs his neck, "You better go, Ann." John looks away and remembers his dad hanging lights up in the trees. He made John and Joseph go out late at night to rake. Esau hid behind the trees and when they would get near a tree while raking Esau jumped out and hit them with the belt. *"Took us a long time to rake the leaves, dad was pure evil that night."* John blinks and comes back to the moment to hear Charles talking.

Charles pleads with Ann, "C'mon, Ann. Just this once. In the same moment he is talking to Ann he remembers Esau yelling at them. *"Get in the house, now."* They didn't move fast enough so he grabbed Charles by his ear and lifted him onto the porch. The ground was three feet below the porch. *"Gosh he tore my earlobe that day and made it bleed. He didn't stop either until he walked me all the way up. Ann better go."*

Charles with an anxious demeanor says, "Dad wants to try out the new motor powered boat. It's gonna be cool, c'mon."

"I said no, you're not gonna convince me." Ann crosses her arms. "I've had enough of him."

Charles tries to calm her "He's not far from here, Ann. Don't get us hit, *please*." Though he's sprouted in the past six months, his body hasn't caught up to the size of his head.

"What's goin' on in here?" Esau stands at the doorway in typical bully fashion.

Butch says, "We're talkin' about the cool new boat you bought and how we all can't wait to ride in it."

Ann had her arms crossed and was looking away unresponsively.

"Y'all better go pack your things we're gonna take advantage of this day. Since it's teacher's day for you, I took a personal day. We can start the weekend off with a boatin' trip."

Ann goes up to her room in silence at the same time the others split.

Twenty minutes went by and Esau is pacing like a ferocious lion on the prowl. "I could be smokin' my new pipe. Call me when she's done pouting, Elsie." Esau storms into his room to get his new pipe. "Gonna pay Prince Albert a visit."

Esau felt wealthy when he smoked his Briar pipe. He listened carefully to the lunch and locker room conversations about pipe smoking. He learned from his buddies at work the aging process was of utmost importance in bringing out the finest smoking qualities. He heard the Briar pipe was known for the economic, careful curing and aging process.

Elsie shakes her head, "I don't know why you gotta always smoke in the house."

Esau taunts, "I'm the man of this house. I bring in the money and I can buy and do what I want. I read in a cigar catalogue if I allow the pipe to age just right it would breathe; take in the wetness and oil from the tobacco, makin' it a cool and dry smoke."

"Yeah, well you can get that kinda smoke outside too."

"Don't sass me woman. I paid a lot of money for this. Let me school you a bit. See this here bowl? Once the curing is done, and the bowls are shaped, they're fitted with mouthpieces, hand finished, stained, polished and waxed." Knowing all of this, made him feel affluent. He filled the bowl with his favorite brand, Prince Albert. He studied his pipe every time he took a puff. He was seated in his favorite recliner and had everyone leave for him to enjoy his smoke.

Elsie gives him a disapproving look.

Esau yelling up, "Ann what's takin' you so long? You're wastin' the day away."

When he didn't get a response, he cussed under his breath. Elsie felt tension and pressure. She began yelling for the kids to go outside, "Stay outside until I call you-ins back in."

He kept working on breaking in his new pipe. He would tamp and relight as often as necessary; and wasn't afraid of using too many matches.

"Don't leave those matches layin' around."

Esau gives Elsie an annoyed look.

If Esau's pipe got too hot, he let it rest awhile then he would pack the dead ashes and relight. He would test if the pipe is too hot by placing it against his cheek like an enthusiast. Esau feels Elsie's condemning eyes on him and fidgets.

"Ann," He calls. He sucks on the pipe and lets out a puff.

Esau still hears nothing and heads to the stairs. "You made me get up off my recliner, you better get down here."

Still silence. He leans forward to start going upstairs.

"You better answer me or I'll come in there and get you."

"I ain't goin', dad." She objects from her room.

"Yes you are you better get your butt out here or I'm gonna beat it."

"I'm not goin' stop tellin' me I am."

"You ungrateful, stupid kid."

He pounds on the door.

Ann jumps up startled but doesn't open the door.

Elsie goes into the living room yells up to Esau, "Leave her alone, she don't wanna go."

He goes back downstairs, sits in his recliner and starts picking on Elsie.

"She's like her stupid, grandma Novak. She always wants to stay home. Your mother is stupid. She ain't shy. She's just a snob with a cob up her..."

"Stop talking about my mother that way, Esau."

"Your mom ain't the special person you all make her to be. She don't wanna help you, she just wants to meddle in our family. That meddling no good bi..."

"Don't you finish that sentence or I'll make you eat that pipe."

"You're just as stupid as she is, Elsie. You're both fat and lazy. You ain't goin' nowhere in life...you're just like her. You're a big scaredy cat, you don't wanna go nowhere. You're always nervous. You're gonna be fat and ugly like her."

"Shut-up, Esau."

"Your mother let herself go. Look at you; you're getting *huge* like her. She's worthless. You're worthless." Esau is cackling louder and louder every time Elsie's shade of red gets brighter on her skin. "Why don't you go live with her again huh? She's a no good for nothing piece of..."

Elsie charges Esau, grabs the pipe and shoves it farther into his mouth and into his throat making him gag on it.

"Gack," Esau's eyes are protruding in shock. He pulls the pipe out of his mouth, "What the..."

Elsie walks out of the room justified in her actions with an indignant strut. "That'll learn ya."

Esau realizes she isn't going to back down. He doesn't want to ruin what may be his last chance at reconciling the marriage. He redirects his intimidating energy towards Ann. He puts out his pipe, lays it down and bounds up the stairs.

He tries to open Ann's door but it's locked. He pounds on it again, "Get out here now."

He's so angry spit is forming at the sides of his mouth.

Elsie is reeling from her confrontation with Esau but knows he is angrier than before. She gives herself some protection by calling the children back inside. They are now waiting downstairs sensing the apprehension in the house, afraid for Ann and ultimately themselves.

"Open this door *right now*."

Elsie hears Esau ranting and yells upstairs, "She can stay home, Esau. Leave her alone."

Ann is shaking, *"Oh please, mommy. Save me from him, please."*

"Over my dead body she is. I took a personal day and she's comin' with us. You stay outta this."

Elsie goes into the kitchen. "You kids want a snack before we leave?"

Butch says, "I'll take that big red tomato, we grew, with salt."

Elsie warns, "You know you ain't supposed to eat those vegetables, they're for your dads work buddies."

"But we're the ones growin' em in the garden. It takes so long. That's not fair."

"Well it makes him feel good about himself when they like 'em at work. Heard your dad sayin' they all think your vegetables are the best. I guess you're doin' a good job. Feel good about *that*."

"Y'all start school back up on Monday and it's my last chance to take you anywhere, get out here now Ann." Esau has worked himself up into a tirade. He paces back and forth again desperate to get Ann out of the room. "I can't believe you're ignoring me like this you disrespectful, no good..."

He pounds on the door with a growl.

"You don't open the door this second I'm gonna knock it down and you'll get what's coming, Ann."

"Oh God, he's gonna kill me."

Ann gets up to unlock the door.

Esau opens the door and leaves it open so the others could hear what happens when a child disobeys.

Butch looks at John. John looks back at him. Charles understands their feelings and the message they are sending to each one with their eyes. They exchange a certain dejected look between them. They want to voice their opinions but knowing that in doing so may provoke a worse beating than the one they're going to get when Ann refuses to go. They want to protect their sister but know how volatile Esau is particularly since he always threatens them with his gun. His firearm was his steal courage and if he was ever vulnerable to his growing sons, he would make sure to show them the intimidating object.

He unbuckles his belt saying, "We'll see about you staying." He slowly slides the belt out of each loop to make a statement and lets it backlash when he reaches the end.

Esau fuming like a crazed lunatic begins beating Ann with the belt. He pushes her over onto her stomach and starts lashing the back of her legs. "I told you…" *Whip*. "…to listen to me…" *Whip*. "But no…" *Whip* "You made me do this to you," He yells.

She tries covering her legs with her hands but he wrestles with her and continues on her back. "No don't…stop," She yells feeling the sting.

She's afraid to turn over because she doesn't want him to hit her face. She has seen how Esau punches Elsie's stomach too.

"You're goin' on that boat trip if I have to beat you all day."

Ann is crying and livid, "No, I'm not goin' I don't care what you say. You're not havin' your way with me anymore. I'm done with you."

"I'll show you done." He whips her again.

He continues whipping her harder and harder.

She screams with every lash, *"Mommy, why aren't you doing something about this? Why won't anyone come up here to stop him?"*

"I'm gonna break you, you're gonna go."

Ann is lifeless and whimpering. She stings all over, *"How old do I hafta be before he stops. Will he ever?"*

With every lash the belt makes a loud, *Whack, Whack*, "You don't go this time, you're goin' the next time and I'm gonna make sure you do what I say *and* what I want."

# Chapter 32

# *Back to school*

The following Monday Ann took her duffle bag with extra clothes for her after school job. She decided to do the total opposite of what she had done. Ann planned to attend all of her classes. Her first and favorite class was shop class because she loved working with wood, making projects. She was good at learning the different sizes of the drill bits and how to cut the pieces perfectly. This project was an owl she would get to put suet in for wild birds.

"Alright class let's continue your projects, this one is worth half of your grade for the semester. You will be graded on preciseness, neatness, attitude, following directions and all the things on the list in front of you." Ann adjusts her protective goggles to look at the list.

The teacher walks around the room with a clipboard observing the student's work. "I like your work, Ann. Outstanding, very neat."

After she got all the parts cut out and sanded, she decided she wanted to paint her project in neutral colors so it can blend in. *"I have to keep workin' or I'll lose my mind thinkin' about what's goin' to happen to me next."* She looked at the clock and first period was flying by. She heard the second hand ticking while everyone concentrated on their projects.

She walked through the hallways looking at blurs of faces, looking beyond the other students and teachers resolute to carry out her plan. The girls were holding their books in a nurturing manner to their chests. The boys held their books in a more detached way tucked under their arms to their sides.

There is a young man with a letterman's jacket walking backwards speaking to another, "Meet me after school, we can do homework at my house."

She turns to unlock her locker to get books for her next classes. *"Oh good, at least math is next."*

A student walks by, "Hi, Ann." She was one of the few students who greeted Ann. Once in a while she would invite Ann to church or to do homework, she knew how smart Ann was. Ann never said yes because she wasn't allowed to have friends outside of school. She wanted to go but said she was busy. The girl knew most of the school made fun of her and her family for being from Virginia. She liked Ann and never saw her as poor but as a sweet girl who was as smart as she was shy.

Ann is in her own thoughts and doesn't notice the greeting; she turns around to head to class. She goes to math and, like the math whiz she is, she gets all the answers right on the test without hardly having to study very much. She breezes through Algebra and is ready for more complex mathematics. She turns her paper over and raises her hand as if she were in a contest. The teacher smiles at her and signals for her to come forward to put her paper in the designated bin. She often fantasized about going to college but she knew she didn't have the resources. Teachers liked her and knew she was hard working yet none of them knew the mayhem she had to suffer at home.

Lunch came, Ann made sure to sit alone. She started to hear conversations around her.

"I'll trade your peanut butter sandwich, candy bar and soda for my turkey smothered in gravy and floating peas, with yummy applesauce and milk on the side," A student laughed.

The other responded, "Yuck, man. No way."

Ann wasn't in a talking mood. She packed her usual boloney sandwich, with cheese and mustard only. When she finished her sandwich she pulled out a crispy sweet apple and began munching on it. The crowded room served as a setting to her thoughts. With each bite she trailed off in a daze remembering the children's book she read as a child. She reminisced about the day she had shared with her grandmother of where she wanted to travel and the places she wanted to go. *"First Israel, and Africa, then some other countries too. I'll fly in a plane. I'll open a business so I can go to these places."*

It seemed like minutes before the bell rang and it was time for her next class. She started to get butterflies in her stomach because she knew the time for her plan was approaching. In a single file, the teenagers militantly align themselves, putting their lunch trays away. Others, throwing away their empty lunch sacks. They're pushing out of the room trying to make it to their next class.

She walks into her history class. She reads the homework assignment on the board and writes it down, *"Hmm, 250 word essay. Bonus points for extra words up to 500."* Although Ann enjoyed reading and hearing the stories, she couldn't focus on what the teacher said. She was preoccupied with the plan she would carry out in a moment.

"I wrote the assignment on the board class," The teacher yells over the students talking in between lessons. "Listen up." She has a protector over the chalk so it doesn't leave her fingers dusty. "All this week we are taking history class to a new level. We'll be doing current history. I know a few of you have family in the Vietnam War, I thought it would be interesting to hear a report to educate us. I want an essay written, all the instructions are on the chalk board."

Ann snaps out of her distraction for a moment, *"Evan is in Vietnam. I hope he's doing alright."*

The bell rang and she was off like a horse at the races. She ran to her locker to get her bag. She went into the bathroom stall to change into her clothes. She ran out and made sure plenty of adults were around when she started to empty the trash cans.

Ann emptied one garbage can into the cart she was pushing, *"I gotta remember to put a fresh bag at the bottom like he taught me."*

"Make sure to keep a fresh bag at the bottom to make it easier for the next..."

When she looks up she hears a loud gasp, paralyzed, she keeps looking forward.

The janitor was a gentle, kind, older man that worked this job after retirement to keep busy. His home was always swarmed with children and grandchildren he could never get enough of them. He had seen many things in his day but what he saw this moment took his breath away.

Ann hears him but is afraid to turn around. *"I wonder if he'll say anything."*

The janitor saw black and blue bruises, and dark maroon colored welts all over the back of Ann's legs. She wore shorts to her job that day. He was appalled and knew those marks were not self-inflicted because they were on the posterior part of her legs. Some bruises were overlapped and dark still others were purple contusions that almost left grooves. Most were raised, red and swollen. He didn't know whether to get indignant or cry so he did both. Almost every portion of her legs were covered in blemishes, blisters and belt marks. He didn't dare make her turn around to see if she had any on her front side. This was enough for him to take action.

Ann continued taking out the overflowing trash bag, tying it up and replacing it with a new bag she left at the bottom from the previous time. She hadn't found the courage to turn around.

The janitor went inside. He picked up the phone book to call child services. His hand was shaking with concern as he was looking to find the number. When he began to explain to the agency what he saw he got choked up and had to regain his composure. He pulled out the handkerchief from his back pocket and wiped his eyes.

Within minutes an agent arrives to the school to take Ann home. *"The plan worked, I'm finally free."*

The case worker is a plain looking woman in her late thirties. Her hair is pulled back in a low pony tail. She is wearing a pant suit and speaks with firmness most times. She's wearing tinted glasses. She addresses the janitor with a solid handshake, "I'm Erica Engle, Ann's case worker." She shows the janitor her I.D. "Thank you for reporting this sir; I will take it from here."

The janitor hugs Ann gently with watery eyes, "God bless you, Ann." He's wearing striped blue overalls like a train engineer. He has a round belt hook of what looked like one hundred keys for every door on the school campus. His hair was snowy white and every wrinkle told a tale he often liked to share with Ann when they worked together. "You have a great work ethic. You're going to be a hard worker when you grow up—and so honest too."

Ann is grateful and although she is touched she has learned to suppress her emotions. "Thank you, sir."

Erica guides Ann into the backseat of her car. "Be careful getting in."

Ann winces trying not to be vocal, *"ow, these welts hurt with shorts on."*

Erica scribbles a few things down on her clipboard. She is almost mechanical but on the inside she is disturbed by the welts and bruises on Ann's legs. She is being professional, trying to remain unbiased.

She accompanies Ann inside her home. After a few hours of investigating she tells Elsie, "Ma'am we have to remove her from this home."

Elsie knows this is what's best for Ann. She appears to be apathetic not wanting to break down in front of everyone. She turns and walks away.

Esau says sneering, "Go ahead and take her. She'll be back. She needs me."

Erica senses his malice. *"I hope they change these laws someday to make people like you accountable, otherwise you people will keep doing this and getting away with it."* She remains composed and impartial. She takes Ann by the arm and escorts her to the car. "Watch your head and please put your seatbelt on, Ann." She has a daughter Ann's age and guards her with her life. Ann's abuse is unfathomable to her.

Ann looks in the rearview mirror, "You believe me, don't you?"

"I do, you're safe now." She adjusts her mirror and smiles at Ann.

"How does someone get away with so much? I've tried to escape before and keep getting sent back home. How do you know I'm safe?"

"We have proof this time; I took plenty of Polaroid's of your bruises and..." She clears her throat trying not to get emotional, "Ahem, of your injuries. Some of them will be turned over to the police."

"Why did he think he could keep doing this?" Ann knew her case worker was familiar with this behavior. She wanted answers.

"I know you want answers, Ann. We'll do our best to help you relocate and be safe. My own grandma went through a lot. She taught me so much. I guess it's why I do what I do. She used to say, 'Abusers always want to be in control of their victims because their minds are out of control'."

Ann looks back at her house, "I guess it makes sense."

Grandma also said, "Once they break you, they figure; *you can't break a willing heart nor can you steal from a giving soul.*" Erica puts the idling car in gear and drives off.

Still struggling to look back at her fading house she says softly, "Your grandma is smart. So, you do this because of your grandma?"

"Every time a girl like you is rescued, it feels like I go back in time and rescue my grandma over and over."

Erica is slowly merging onto the road, "Grandma didn't have someone like me or a voice like you. When you grow up it'll be improved. You have a voice, Ann. Your story can save lives, just like grandmas. She says *all things* work for good."

"Now I understand what *my* grandma was trying to tell me," Ann says.

The car drives off with Ann never to return home. As she's watching her house get smaller and smaller, her chest aching with pain, but her future hopeful with joy, she turns around and looks forward.

*"I promise to give my story a voice someday. Maybe it'll save some lives."*

# Chapter 33

# *Pictures*

H e pulls a gun on the nursing home administrator. "Which hand do you write with? Gonna shoot that one first."

He aims at the administrator's foot, "Which foot is your favorite to lean on? That one's next."

"That's It Mr. Flink I don't care if you're a 75 year old man visiting your wife in a nursing home, you have no right to threaten another life with a gun."

"Y'all won't lemme see my wife, Gretta who's in here."

"You've been cruel to her, Mr. Flink. We can't allow you to continue being mentally and emotionally abusive to her. It's inexcusable."

The administrator, Michael Brent, picked up the telephone receiver and dialed. He was wearing a business suit with a white starched shirt and gold plated cuff links. His light blue paisley tie matched the handkerchief tucked in his left front breast pocket. He pushed up his glasses from the side. He was in his mid-forties. He looked laid back until his buttons were pushed and he became a *play by the rules type.* He was new to this position but already had many complaints about Esau. Esau's stunt was the final straw. He wasn't going to take any more.

Esau with a sheepish grin says, *"Go ahead."*

Michael looks into Esau's gray eyes which were once brown. The color deteriorated each year like his character. "Yes, Susan I know you are Esau's case worker. He's committed a crime by pulling a gun on me just now. I'm going to have to call the police. I already told him politely several times he wasn't allowed in here but he came back with a gun. You can meet him at the police station. You had better go talk to him before we slap him with sexual harassment and stalking charges too."

The smell of freshly brewed coffee and food saturated the air signaling lunch time. It was mixed with the sterile cleaning products used in every room and in the hallways.

Michael spins his leather chair around, his back is towards Esau, "Well he may not treat you that way but once he's no longer in control, he's dangerous. You need to take care of this."

Michael whirls his chair back around and calls the police. He waits for an officer to come take his report. The administrator bangs the phone down to show he's fearless. *"God I hope he wasn't really going to go through with it."*

Esau says, "I can't believe you just called the law you, idiot. I was just messin' w…"

"That's assault with a deadly weapon, it's more than *messin.*" He put his fingers up in quotations with the last word.

Esau with absolute sarcasm rolls his eyes.

"You *will* be doing time for this, I assure you."

With a mocking look Esau says, "Why did you tell her about sexual harassment and stalkin'?"

"We have several reports from the aids and nurses you've been making unwanted advances towards them."

"It's just candy and flirting. I hardly say that's stalkin'. 'Sides, I ain't never been in trouble with the law."

"No, Mr. Flink you just haven't been caught. You can't follow aids and nurses to their homes. You can't make sexual advances towards them either. You're no longer welcomed here, Mr. Flink. Your wife Gretta has declined to see you anymore."

"Gretta is stupid. I can find one half her age that'll make babies with me. A virgin too if I want."

"Things have a way of catching up to us, Mr. Flink. If you continue on this path there is no telling where your future will lead."

Susan Rossford was a young case worker who was new on the job. Completely unaware of his secreted past or his dangerous tendencies, she persisted in finding a family member who would care for him. With a blind optimism she dials the phone. She begins to call everyone in Esau's family. Everyone's phone rings and she leaves several messages for them to call her back. She is unrelenting until only one phone is answered when she makes her second round of calls.

Ann is 50, sitting in her kitchen organizing her photo album, cataloguing her trips to the aspired places of her dreams. She wasn't disappointed at how small Israel was like many who first go, but was inspired by the layers of history that sculpted her own life. Her commitment to the One who walked its roads was the sanctuary she went to at every experience of her life. She knew her identity wasn't what she lived but why and who she lived for.

She gets up to grind whole coffee beans to brew. A mill grinder is preferable to her because all the coffee is ground to a level she liked. After her desired consistency she begins to brew the perfect pot of coffee. Her favorite peanut butter cookies are on a plate near the pot.

She hears the phone ring and leans over to see *Department of Corrections* on the caller I.D. She can't begin to imagine who it is or what they want. It goes over to voicemail on her answering machine because she has her hands full brewing coffee. *"I can call back."*

"Hi, I'm Susan Rossford from the Department of Corrections. I'd like to speak with you about a family member. Please call me at 888-555-5522."

"Hmm, I wonder who that could be," Ann takes a sip of her hot cup of dark brewed coffee.

She is organizing photographs of West Bank, Tel Aviv, Jerusalem, Golan Heights, Gaza Strip and boat rides on the Sea of Galilee and its imposing mountains. She is looking at pictures of the lengthy coastal plain. She remembers the intimidating rockets in Sdirot that flew over her head. She thinks of walking the ramparts of Old Jerusalem seeing Israel's natives living within the walls. She has a mental snapshot of the Wailing Wall when she cried praying the *Kaddish* in the presence of the Divine. She wore the customary headdress out of respect. Her friends sent *tzetzels* to be placed as prayers in the cracks of the wall to be heard by the ears of God. Her greatest moment was being baptized in the Jordan River.

Ann frequented Africa and looks at her pictures from Mozambique, South Africa, Kenya, and Uganda where she still supports two young girls so they can go to a Christian school. She receives letters, school grades and updated photos every year from them. Her support allows them to get an education they otherwise wouldn't be able to afford. She had stills of speaking to some of the tribes. She had some Polaroid's given to her by the team she was with while they handed out clothing and basic necessities to the community. She saw dancing, laughter, hugs, tears, and stunning colors painted on their bodies that almost came to life when Ann held the pictures.

She looked at the photos of her children and grandchildren as they posed with the souvenirs she had brought back from each location. She giggled at the pictures she took with some of the pilots and stewardesses when they gave her some airline pins with wings. She returned from her trips with silver packets of peanuts for her family.

She chuckled at the picture of the frantic woman that lost her passport in Frankfurt, Germany on a trip home where they all thought they would be stranded during a layover. After an hour of hysteria she remembered she placed them in her friend's purse so she wouldn't lose them.

Ann smiled as she saw the images from Guatemala and the Dominican Republic when she went as a missionary and construction worker on behalf of her own company of which she is CEO. She gazes at pictures of the rugged land of mountains, beautiful lakes, and lush vegetation, which at the time was in a long and brutal civil war. It was among the ten poorest countries in Latin America. The distribution of income remained unequal and poverty was prevalent. Often the government would allow missionaries to alleviate the despair. As missionaries her team handed out rations in rural areas and among the poorly educated. Malnutrition among Guatemalan children was high, as was mortality. *"These people taught me so much. If I can save just one."*

Many of the indigenous people in those countries spoke Mayan. Ann remembered some of the words she learned. *Ba'ax ka wa'alik* which meant *"hello"* or *"how are you doing?"* Ann loved the unique opportunity to minister among the groups that surrounded the area. She took every chance she could to share the One she had experienced herself. She became close to the natives who were bilingual and helped her communicate.

Her smile was a feeling of hopefulness to her imminent return to those places. Absorbed in her photos she is startled by the sudden ring that brings her back from her reminiscing. Her heart pounds as she walks towards the phone in a slow and uneasy walk. She looks at the caller I.D., again it says, *Department of Corrections*, "Hello?"

# Epilogue

Present day, Ann is now 54. Although she experienced an encounter with God at an early age she gave her life to Him at age 7. Prayer was the thread weaving throughout her childhood, keeping her together, giving her the strength to survive. The events in this novel are true based on Ann's memory. As you read in the last chapter, Ann built her own remodeling company from the ground up. She is currently the CEO. With this God given talent, she was able to travel to the places she fantasized about in her book. She supports charitable causes with her donations. She has been to different countries, speaking of her experiences with different missionaries. She has three children and six grandchildren.

Ann has finally come to accept the fact her earthly father may never change. She is grateful her Heavenly Father, who has always been there for her, will never change.

The point of view character Ann, is based on a real person. This book is based on true events, however all names appearing in this work are fictitious. Names and locations have been changed to protect the characters the book is based on. An author has embellished some events given by her coauthor.

## Sisters

Like intricate lines,
our lives defined...
...chosen each day to intertwine.
Some days are menial,

Some days are timed.
Other days are complicated
and others...Divine.
You make one move
I make a line.
You make one more
I take my time...
but in the end
we always find,
we're two separate beings,
two separate lines.
Is there such a thing as an uneven line?
Only if by lines, our lives defined.
If you go your way, and I go mine
We'll always reconnect
Our lives, our lines.

—LL—

## Book Discussion Guide by: Leanette Lopez

Author: Leanette Lopez is also a recording artist and speaker. For more information and bookings please visit www.leanettelopez.com

Coauthor S.L. Miles for whom the story is based on can be found on www.slmiles.com

### Chapter 1 *The Chicken Coop*

For Ann the chicken coop is a symbol of abuse. Is there a chicken coop in your life?

### Chapter 2 *Hurricane*

*Elsie notices the strange nervousness of Ann's demeanor as a tinge of red covers the light freckles on her face. Elsie scrutinizes the menacing look by Esau but looks the other way.* What do these lines in chapter 2 mean to you?

Chapter 3 *Remodeling*

Why and or how does a story like this help people?

Chapter 4 *Love Thy Neighbor*

In love or in lust...how can you tell the difference? Have you been there?

Chapter 5 *Romanticize*

Darla clearly has daddy issues. How do you fulfill needs without compromising who you are?

Chapter 6 *Withholding*

One type of seductive withholding is when the with-holder enjoys toying with others because it gives them excitement. Most lack any kind of consideration for those they seduce then discard.

How do you recognize this type of personality? How would you deal with it?

Chapter 7 *Sisters*

What would you do if you had a family member or friend go through domestic violence?

## Chapter 8 *The Only Way Out*

Elsie has a meltdown. Does anyone think it was post partum depression or something more severe?

## Chapter 9 *Child's Play*

What do you do for fun as an adult? How important is it to take time to play?

## Chapter 10 *Tree House*

Many people who suffer abuse as children learn to disassociate and avoid close relationships. How does this affect them as adults?

## Chapter 11 *Hikey*

When my coauthor gave me the info of things they did as children...I wasn't intentional about having the fingernail growing scene follow the hikey scene. Every time I read through it, I laughed. (On a serious note, did you notice how Ann & Sadie want to talk about the abuse but don't.)

## Chapter 12 *Following Signs and Wonders*

Why do you think the change in Esau and Elsie was temporary?

## Chapter 13 *No More Cancer*

Do you believe in miracles?

## Chapter 14 *Tomboy*

At any time, is it appropriate for children to be involved in adult issues?

## Chapter 15 *Midwife*

Do you share your faith at work? If so, is there a tactful way of doing it?

## Chapter 16 *Dog Chain*

Elsie stands up for herself. Was it the best way to do it?

## Chapter 17 *How Far Down is Up*

Who or what inspires you?

## Chapter 18 *Panic Attack*

This is a personal chapter for me. I learned to disarm panic attacks in this manner...it happened throughout childhood and early adulthood. Have you ever had a panic attack? Are you embarrassed to say it right now? (I was embarrassed, I assure you, you are not alone).

## Chapter 19 *Rodeo Roundup*

The children stand up for themselves. What did you think about this chapter?

## Chapter 20 *Hog*

We all have funny stories, what's yours?

## Chapter 21 *Sadie & Martha*

Do you have a friendship as close as a sibling?

## Chapter 22 *Just Stay Away*

Is denial the answer?

## Chapter 23 *Death of a Spirit*

We are not sure if Esau followed through with his threats to Sadie but Ann & Miriam's memories were written in this chapter. How do you feel about encouraging children to tell?

## Chapter 24 *Mad For You*

I had a counselor friend tell me that everyone who goes through abuse should have someone mad for them. When I realized who that person was for my life, I went to them, told them my story, and was free. Do you have someone to get mad for you?

### Chapter 25 *Making Up*

Abusers go through the *honeymoon* phase perpetuating a sense of normalcy for the abused. How does one break away?

### Chapter 26 *When Innocence Encounters Evil*

Would you ever take a person's sudden change in personality as a sign? Would you act on it?

### Chapter 27 *Fishing*

Esau tries to save Evan. What is the difference between natural instinct and truly caring?

### Chapter 28 *Trip to the Store*

Have you ever had to pay the piper?

### Chapter 29 *Bikes*

How do you teach children work ethic?

### Chapter 30 *Driving Lessons*

Do you think filling potholes raised any questions between the boys?

## Chapter 31 *Boating*

This is the climax to the story where Ann decides to escape. Is there an easier way in today's society?

## Chapter 32 *Back to School*

The social worker was passionate about saving children. What are you passionate about?

## Chapter 33 *Pictures*

Do you want to share any fond memories?

## Epilogue

Both coauthor and I had an epiphany while writing this book. Hers was with her father, mine was a different relationship. We came to terms with the fact we are incapable of giving unconditional love to people who will continue to manipulate or take from us. As Christians we are taught to love regardless but in conversation with a close friend, he told me I wasn't wired like God to love unconditionally without getting hurt every time. His advice to me was, "Sometimes you have to love from afar." Do you agree with this statement?

## Domestic Violence Resources

If someone you know is in an abusive relationship —
or if that someone is you — there are places you can
turn for help. The following is a list of resources for
victims of domestic violence:

## National Domestic Violence Hotline:

(800) 799-SAFE (7233)
or 800.787.3224 (TTY)
www.ndvh.org

## National Network to End Domestic Violence

(202) 543-5566
www.nnedv.org

## American Psychiatric Association (APA)

(703) 907-7300
www.healthyminds.org

## National Coalition against Domestic Violence

Phone: (202) 745-1211
Phone: (303) 839-1852
Fax: (202) 745-0088
Fax: (303) 831-9251
www.ncadv.org

## The National Center for Victims of Crime

(202) 467-8700
www.ncvc.org

## The Family Violence Prevention Fund

(415) 252-8900
FAX: (415) 252-8991
www.endabuse.org

## National Resource Center on Domestic Violence

(800) 537-2238
FAX: (717) 545-9456
www.nrcdv.org

## The Battered Women's Justice Project

TOLL-FREE: (800) 903-0111 ext. 3
Phone: (215) 351-0010
FAX: (215) 351-0779
www.bwjp.org

## National Battered Women's Law Project

Phone: (212) 741-9480
FAX: (212) 741-6438

## National Women's Health Information Center

(800) 994-9662
www.4women.gov

## The Domestic Violence and Mental Health Policy Initiative

(312) 726-7020
www.dvmhpi.org

## National Teen Dating Abuse Helpline

www.loveisrespect.org
(866) 331-9474

## Safe Place

www.safeplace.org
(512) 267-SAFE

## Break the Cycle

www.breakthecycle.org

## Rape Abuse and Incest National Network (RAINN)

(800) 656-HOPE
www.rainn.org

## Health Resource Center on Domestic Violence

Phone: (800) 313-1310
FAX: (415) 252-8991

*If you believe you need immediate assistance, please call your local emergency number or the mental health crisis hotline listed in your local phone book's government pages. Because neither of the authors do not operate, supervise, or exercise any control over any of the therapists, resources or referral services listed, it makes no representations or warranty what-soever, either expressed or implied, regarding any information or advice provided by these referral services. In no event shall it, nor either of the authors be liable to you or anyone else for any decision made or action taken in reliance on information provided by these therapists, resources or referral services.*

CPSIA information can be obtained at www.ICGtesting.com
Printed in the USA
LVOW082150161111

255368LV00007B/12/P